Praise for *Close Encounters of a Third-World Kind*

"Stewart writes with humor and just the right amount of sarcasm to appeal to young readers. Not only does she demonstrate an understanding of a twelve-year-old girl trying to deal with a bratty younger sister while trying very hard to grow up, she also describes the appeal of an adventure in a country that changes her life forever."
—*Language Arts*

"The story is humorous yet the problems of life in an underdeveloped country, such as the lack of medical care and education, are woven in unobtrusively.... This light-hearted book will lead readers into a totally different kind of life from their own." —*School Library Journal*

"Stewart. . . provides realistically appealing detail about Annie's life-changing experience, and messages about cultural difference are delivered quietly and authentically.... This one manages to bring genuine good humor to this story of an eye-opening journey." —*The Bulletin*

"Full of local color and snippets of cultural information, the comedy-adventure will surely please." —*Kirkus Reviews*

Florida Sunshine State Young Reader's Award Master List
Black-Eyed Susan Book Award Nominee
Connecticut Nutmeg Book Award Nominee
Grand Canyon Reader Award Nominee
Teddy Children's Book Award Finalist

CLOSE ENCOUNTERS

OF A

THIRD-WORLD

KIND

BY

Jennifer J. Stewart

Holiday House / New York

Acknowledgments

My queen of editors at Holiday House, Regina Griffin, helped shape this book, and the two before it. Long may she reign! Hugs also to my writing friends: C. S. Adler, Patricia McCord, Marianne Mitchell, and Janni Lee Simner.

5   7   9   10   8   6   4

Library of Congress Cataloging-in-Publication Data

Stewart, Jennifer J.
Close encounters of a third-world kind / by Jennifer J. Stewart.—1st ed.
p. cm.
Summary: Twelve-year-old Annie is reluctant to travel to a village in Nepal for her father's two-month medical mission, but once there she assists at the clinic, makes friends with a local girl, and has adventures that change her life.
ISBN 0-8234-1850-2 (hardcover)
[1. Medical care—Fiction. 2. Sex role—Fiction. 3. Friendship—Fiction.
4. Missionaries—Fiction. 5. Nepal—Fiction.] I. Title.

PZ7.S84895Cl 2004
[Fic]—dc22
2003067601
ISBN-13: 978-0-8234-1850-3
ISBN-13: 978-0-8234-2161-9 (paperback)

For my husband,
who took us there

Contents

CLOSE
ENCOUNTERS
OF A THIRD-WORLD
KIND

Chapter 1

Up in the Air

I saw a plane like it in a museum once, suspended by cables from the ceiling. Someone famous had flown it. Now its evil twin glittered on the runway.

"We're flying in *that?*" Fear glued the soles of my sneakers to the asphalt, and my little sister, Chelsea, bumped into me from behind.

It's not that I'm afraid, but you have to know I'm a 747 kind of girl. I like in-flight magazines and packets of salty pretzels and my choice of soda: root beer, no ice. And did you know barf bags can be turned into really neat puppets?

But I especially like radar.

Dad tugged on the strap of my backpack, towing me forward. "Well, how else do you expect to get to Tumlingtar?" he asked in that reasonable voice of his, as if every day people strap themselves into antique planes and fly off to places no one has heard of.

It could be a bad omen that it is pronounced TOMB-ling-tar, but I am trying not to let that bother me. "I don't know. Walk?" Ha ha, I knew there weren't any roads.

He ignored the question. "Annie, I'm really proud of the way you're adjusting to this. I know it's hard." He gave my shoulder a squeeze. "Think of it as an adventure!"

Yeah, *your* adventure. I'm just along for the ride. But just when I'm ready to admit how scared I am, Dad has to go and compliment me.

Now I had a new mantra. It was better than the Buddhist monks chanting, "*Om Mane Padme Hum*," which chanted fast sounds like "Oh, Mommy, Take Me Home." Unfortunately that wouldn't work; Mom is geared up for adventure with a capital *A*. She had Chelsea by the hand now and they'd bypassed us. Dad cocked an eyebrow at me, waiting. There was nothing to do but climb the aluminum stairs, which folded neatly behind us.

The flight attendant doled out cotton to plug our ears and hard candies to suck on. I stowed my backpack under the seat in front of me. Across the aisle, Dad tried to cram both his feet and his pack under the seat, but only his feet fit.

No one demonstrated the proper use of supplemental oxygen masks or life vests in the event of an emergency, not even how to buckle and unbuckle the seat belt. Dad patted my hand. "Annie, we're not going to be flying high enough to pressurize the cabin, and I don't think we're flying over water," he assured me. "Relax."

Like I could. My brain doesn't work that way. When you say "relax," to me, it's guaranteed that my little gray cells won't be able to. Other people's neurons can lie out in their swimsuits, lazing around at the beach, but mine scan the horizon for shark fins.

It is not that I am the most uptight girl you ever met—that would be my best friend, Kayla—but put it this way: You will never see me sky dive or bungee jump for fun. Heights don't scare me. It's the falling that makes me twitch.

Flying on two itty-bitty propellers and the prayers of its eighteen passengers, the plane groaned when it took off, but the pilots and flight attendant didn't look fazed at all.

However, they believe in reincarnation.

When I opened my eyes, Kathmandu, that strange city that managed to be both modern and medieval, had disappeared. Below me lay a rumpled crazy quilt of a country. Terraces dry as bone stairstepped up hillsides. Houses hunkered down by paths; there were no roads. An ant trail of people headed for a village, a bustling metropolis of about twelve buildings.

Dad was pointing out his window. "Everest," he mouthed above the bumblebee-flying-into-a-headwind noise of the engines. I leaned forward. You know, looking up from an airplane, the snowy tip of the world's tallest mountain jutting out of the clouds isn't so impressive, until you figure out how much of its base lies below them. The rest of the Helping Hearts medical team reached for their cameras. My fingers itched to get its silhouette down on paper, but I could no more draw a straight line than the pilot could fly one. The plane was bouncing up and down like it had hiccups.

"An adventure," I muttered. Then for good measure, "*Om Mane Padme Hum.*" Fast.

I concentrated on keeping lunch inside me, where it belonged.

* * *

Some forty minutes later, Tracey, the dental hygienist who was sitting in front of me, swiveled, her eyes wild. Even with cotton-stuffed ears, I could hear her scream: "We're all going to die!!!" The cockpit didn't have a door, and I could see out the same window the pilots did.

A mountain loomed smack in front of us.

The plane made a slow stomach-wrenching turn, banked sharply, and headed straight down.

Chapter 2

How I Got into This Predicament

They say your whole life can flash in front of you in the time it takes to blink—like a video played at light speed. You would hope someone would edit the tape and cut out the embarrassing parts, like my turn as a singing, dancing carrot who really, really needed to use the bathroom in the second-grade Thanksgiving play. Since the director's cut isn't available, I guess I should explain how I got here.

For twelve years, I had a perfectly normal life. I lived with my parents, Kurt and Sue Ferris, my little sister, Chelsea (who I could do without), and my dog, Frisbee (who is more essential). Frizz gives my face a lick every morning when my alarm goes off. It sounds gross, but I like it.

Well, I only thought we were normal.

This past Christmas morning, surrounded by crumpled wrapping paper and wearing sticky bows on our heads, my dad announced that he wanted to do a medical mission trip and take us with him. I had trouble taking him seriously. Being bald, he had the most bows.

"What's that?" I ask, my mouth full of cookies Santa had left behind.

"It's when you go to another country and are a doctor to poor people," Mom explained, the way she does so that even a five-year-old—that would be Chelsea—will get it. Dad teaches at the College of Medicine, and he had a sabbatical coming up. That means the college will pay him to work somewhere else. He says he wants to get back to his medical roots, which apparently he can do best in a third-world country that has never heard of HMOs. And Mom, who quit her job and threw out all her panty hose when Chelsea was born, says she's about due for a sabbatical, too.

Notice no one asks me if I want one. Now the Swiss Army knife weighing down the toe of my Christmas stocking makes sense.

My parents expect me to leave behind my friends and my faithful dog, who will probably forget all about me because she's actually not all that intelligent. I'll miss two months of school, which doesn't really bother me, and, besides, it is educational to go to some country where they eat yak cheese.

Really.

Even with that hint about the world's tallest mountain, most people don't have a clue where we're going. Get out an atlas and head for Asia. That's right, the continent. Then look above India and below China. A string bean of a country, Nepal is south of Tibet. On a globe, you have to walk your fingers to the other side of the earth, as far away as you can get from the United States. It's that remote.

It took months to get ready: buying gear we'd need, getting shots for exotic diseases we did not want to die from, giving away our token houseplant, also known as the fern that ate Boston. Mom went into full-out list-making mode. Even Chelsea knew to stay out of Mom's way when she started ticking off things.

Here's what a normal trip checklist looks like:

Hats (my mom is big on hats)
Swimsuits
Beach towels
Sunscreen
Masks
Snorkels
Fins

Then we pack only four changes of clothes, because we always stay at a place with a washer and dryer. And, obviously, a beach.

Contrast that with:

Hats
First-aid kit (we are going to be a combina-
    tion walking drugstore and ER)
Hiking boots
Moleskin (it isn't really moleskin; it's for blisters)
Water purifier (I wonder if I can drink soda
    all the time?)
Sleeping bags
Backpacks
Water bottles
Flashlights
Solar battery charger
Etc.

Three pages' worth, it went on and on. Mom says it's not like they have Target or Wal-Mart there if we forget something. We have to take it with us.

But while Mom gets all happy when she's writing lists, because she's thinking of every single possibility, and she's going to be Boy Scout standard prepared thorough, I get worried, because now I'm thinking of every single possibility.

And what I'm thinking is that I'd rather not have to use a lot of the things on her list.

All too soon we stood at the airport, corralled by our duffel bags and duct-taped cardboard boxes filled with donated medical supplies and other essentials (several dozen rolls of toilet paper and many fun-size packages of M&M's). Grandpa had printed KATHMANDU OR BUST on the largest box. He wore sunglasses on his head, ready to flip down over his eyes to pretend Frizz was a guide dog if security objected to her furry presence. (Grandpa reads too many spy novels.) Frizz gave me a lick, Grandpa gave us all one last tickly mustache kiss, and we started on our journey.

If you've read this far, you've probably figured out that the plane didn't do a death spiral, neither the two-day succession of jets we took to get to Nepal, nor the museum piece we sat in now.

Thankfully, instead of crashing, first the prop plane buzzed the grass landing strip to frighten off some loitering goats, then set down bumpily. We had arrived. I unstuck myself from the armrests, fingernail by fingernail, stood up on shaky legs, and filed out after the others.

After her outburst, I thought Tracey would fall to her knees and kiss the ground the way the pope does, but maybe she thought better of it, what with all that goat poop.

She caught my eye and grinned, which looked funny, because you don't see too many grown-ups with braces. "Sorry, Annie," she said, giving my arm a little squeeze. "I don't think anyone else heard me, do you? Can you keep it a secret? I get a little hyper sometimes."

"A little?" No way would I be within a five-mile radius of the woman when she was a lot hyper. "Only, Tracey? You know I'm not sitting behind you on the way back. Because there is no entire way I am ever getting on that plane again."

"Deal." Tracey laughed, but I was serious. "We'll walk back." She sat down and began lacing up her hiking boots. In her ankle length skirt and long-sleeved shirt, she looked at lot like Popeye's girl-friend, Olive Oyl. Mom, Chelsea, and I wore similar outfits. The long skirt felt peculiar, like I'd have to keep kicking it out of my way, and I longed for my hiking pants with the zip-off legs. But Mom says pants aren't appropriate here, unless you have a Y chromosome.

A group of porters in short shorts waited to take our gear, not one of them taller than me, but each with calf muscles bigger than my thighs.

While they were stacking our gear onto doko baskets, piling it taller than Chelsea and roping it securely to hoist onto their backs, Dr. Khadka, the Nepali dentist, slung his backpack over his shoulder and pointed to a faint dust track leading away from the airstrip. "We should be proceeding," he announced. "It is better arriving before dark."

It's going to take that long? is what I thought, but "Why?" is what I asked.

"There are cliffs, Annie," he replied.

As in: to fall off. Silly me. I hurried to finish lacing my boots.

The sun cooked the back of my shirt, but my watch claimed it was past midnight, the day before, because we'd crossed the international date line. Back home, Grandpa and Frisbee would be snoring in stereo. I wondered what Grandpa would do when Frizz gave him a friendly wake-up kiss.

In that movie where Julie Andrews won't stop singing, when she and her new husband and his kids climb ev'ry mountain over the Alps, from Austria to Switzerland, they're all happy, but believe me, I was not. The faint track led past the so-called village—a few scattered houses and dirt-clodded fields—then quickly headed up into the foothills. For the first hour, there wasn't any shade. My boots felt like they weighed five pounds each. Even if chased by Nazis, I couldn't go any faster, and I certainly didn't feel like singing.

I stopped to make a public-service announcement.

"Attention, Dad: This wasn't my idea; I don't want to be here, and could we say I tried it, didn't like it, and can I be excused now?"

Dad wiped his sweaty face with a bandanna and said, "Very funny. Do you have any hot spots you need to put moleskin on?"

I gave him a look I planned to use on him a lot when I turned into a teenager. "My feet are fine," I said. "No blisters. They just don't want to walk anymore."

Chelsea heard me and immediately begged to be carried.

After another hour of torture, Dr. Khadka suggested we stop for refreshment.

I didn't see any restaurant, just a shaky wooden bench beside the path and a mud-colored house a few steps beyond. A woman came out and put her palms together, so that her fingertips grazed the spiky gold ring in her nose. "Namaste," she greeted us, bowing.

We namaste-ed back. It works for both "Hello" and "Good-bye," and means something like "I salute the god within you."

The god within was thirsty.

"Chia," Dr. Khadka called the hot spicy tea. There weren't enough glasses, so we drank it in turns. Naturally, Chelsea got hers first. She glugged it down, then ran after a mother duck and her two fuzzy babies. The woman swished Chelsea's glass in a bucket of water and refilled it for me. The ducks came waddling my way, as fast as they could waddle, followed closely by Chelsea. The woman bent down to grab a duckling and put it in Chelsea's hands. Its head poked out frantically between her fingers, and everyone laughed. The woman smiled. She picked up the other duckling and put it in the bucket. It swam in tight circles, peeping loudly, until Chelsea deposited its sister or brother in with it.

I set my glass down. Germs. Just ducky. Not.

With Dr. Khadka translating, the woman started asking about us. She touched the ends of Chelsea's hair, marveling. (It's true—blondes do have more fun; my dark brown hair got ignored.) Chelsea smiled, playing up the cuteness factor. "You have two daughters?" the woman asked.

"Yes, I have two daughters," Mom answered.

"You have no son?"

Mom acknowledged she was right.

"Maybe next time," the woman said, smiling.

In Nepal, apparently boys are better. You know when people adopt Chinese babies, they are always girls? It's like that.

Welcome to my nightmare.

Now we began climbing in earnest. There weren't many switchbacks or turns; we slogged straight up. Five hours and three packets of M&M's later (Chelsea's share doled out one favorite color at a time to keep her moving), we arrived at the village. No one rushed out to greet us. We skirted the silent buildings. The medical students—Peter, Alicia, Lance, and Rudy—dug headlamps out of their packs. Single file, they could be a well-fed group of dusty miners, heigh-hoing home.

Behind one last building, up one last hill, we stumbled upon two rows of tents. Under an awning barely lit by kerosene lanterns, benches had been pushed up against two long tables. We collapsed onto them.

In short order, cooks set out steaming pots and platters of food and we got into the buffet line. Rice, a thin beany soup to spoon over it, and two yellow kinds of curried vegetables, plus hot water, hot tea, and boiled milk. Mom dished out a little of everything for Chelsea.

Chelsea stared at her plate. "What is it?" She didn't pick up her fork, a bad sign.

"It's called *daal bhat*," Mom told her, putting on her happy face. "It's traditional Nepali food, everybody eats it. Give it a try."

"You'd better, Chelse," I added, "because you're going to be eating a lot of it."

Chelsea used her fork to mix the lentils and rice together. It looked vomitrocious. "We brought peanut butter," she said hopefully.

"I'm not unpacking that now," Mom said. "Try it."

While Dad mixed some cocoa powder into milk, I took an experimental forkful. *Daal bhat* ranked slightly above oatmeal without the brown sugar and blueberries.

Evidently Tracey had read as many guidebooks as Mom because she was telling Chelsea it's the custom to eat with the right hand.

"With my fingers?" Chelsea asked. She didn't wait for the answer, but dug in.

It looked like fun, but not without hand sanitizer.

When we had clanked our stainless steel plates into a large bowl for washing, Dr. Khadka stood up. "Tomorrow we will set up at the hospital. Then we will run clinic in the afternoon." He wished us a good night's rest.

"What am I supposed to do tomorrow?" I asked Mom.

"Oh, you'll help, too," she answered. "Don't worry."

"But, Mom—"

She was busy brushing bits of rice off my sister. "Not now, Annie. Can you help Chelsea find her toothbrush?"

And her pajamas, and the rubber Gila monster she sleeps with—why can't Chelsea do anything for herself?

After using the tent latrine—I was glad it was dark—and brushing my teeth, spitting carefully over the side of the cliff, I zipped myself into the tent, changed into my pajamas, and snuggled into my sleeping bag. Chelsea was already snoring adenoidally beside me, so I couldn't talk to her even if I'd wanted to. At home, I don't have to share a bedroom with her, just the bathroom (she gets stickers from Mom if she remembers flushing is nice). Here, we'd be sharing a tent for the next two months.

Joy.

Maybe I'd had enough adventure already.

Mom and Dad whispered good night through the tent flap. "We're in the next tent over if you need anything," Mom assured me.

Funny, when they leave me to baby-sit, I have the name and phone number of the restaurant they're going to, Dad's digital pager number, Mom's cell phone number, plus Grandpa's old rotary dial phone number as backup. I feel safe. Here, everything was all mixed up and strange. For now, the world had shrunk to the size of the tent floor. When I switched off my flashlight, blackness closed in on me. I couldn't remember it ever being so dark.

I missed my dog.

Though I would never have done it if she'd been awake, I scooted closer to Chelsea. With the wind blowing against the side of the tent closest to me, I slept.

Chapter 3

Welcoming Ceremonies

A cheerful, "Good morning, Miss!" woke me. When I unzipped the tent flap, I found two teenaged guys smiling at the pictures of frogs on my pajamas. Then they poured steaming water from a giant teakettle into basins. "For washing," one said, and handed me the first bowl.

Ignoring the wash water, Chelsea scrambled into her clothes and ran outside to explore. I zipped the tent back up and scrubbed everywhere with a washcloth, glad for double water rations, then dressed and followed.

By day, I could see that the Helping Hearts medical

camp required the entire top of the hill. Though level in the center, the sides dropped off steeply—I would stay away from the edge. Down below, I could make out the lone building we'd passed last night, and beyond that, the village proper. The white building off the main drag had to be the hospital. There the path forked. To the right, there was a large dusty open space. To the left, buildings crowded together. Wherever houses weren't perched, the countryside had been terraced into giant staircases for growing rice. Mountains stole the horizon.

After breakfasting on a fried egg each and hot cereal that looked like Cream of Wheat, but sure didn't taste like it, sluiced down by hot tea laced with sugar and boiled milk, we headed for the hospital. Besides the four of us, our leader, Dr. Khadka the dentist, his able assistant, Tracey, and the medical students, there were a pair of Nepali nurses, Kalpana and Devyani. The porters trailed us, carting boxes of supplies on their backs.

Halfway down the hill, an ebony goat in front of the police station caught Chelsea's attention. She stopped to pet him.

"What is his name?" she asked the skinny police officer.

"Oh, honey, I don't think goats have names here," Mom said.

"Yeah, Chelse—they *eat* them," I told her, watching Chelsea's eyes go buggy. Mom shot me a did-you-have-to-say-that? look.

But the police officer bent down to Chelsea's level. "His name Black Handsome."

"That is a good name," said Chelsea. "He's very handsome." She stroked the goat's ears. I reached out a hand. The fur on the goat's back bristled, but his floppy ears were soft and supple.

That goat would have followed after us like Mary's rascally lamb if the police officer hadn't tugged him back by the horns.

At the bottom of the hill, a girl joined our parade, shadowing Chelsea. She smiled at my mother, namasted her, and held out a bunch of small white flowers tied with string.

"Why, thank you," said Mom, accepting the bouquet. "*Dhaanyabad.*" She had listened to the Nepali language tape over and over, and I think she liked to show off.

Not to be outdone, Dad asked in careful Nepali, "What is your name?"

At first the girl was too shy to answer, or maybe she didn't understand. Dad repeated himself, and she smiled behind the fingers she held to her mouth. He pointed to himself and said, "Kurt." He pointed to Mom and said, "Sue," then did the same with me and Chelsea.

The girl repeated, "Chelsea, Ahnee." Then she said in English, "My name Nirmala," and pointed to herself.

"Nirmala?" my mother asked.

"Nirmala," the girl repeated.

"Wormula," said Chelsea, giggling. She got a look from Mom.

Nirmala wasn't much bigger than Chelsea, but probably two or three years older. (I guess it's all the fortified breakfast cereal we eat.) The girl had on a faded blouse over a dark blue skirt. Its hem was coming unstitched. Like all the Nepali people we'd met, she had dark hair and eyes, and brown skin so smooth it looked polished, not dotted with freckles like mine. Her feet wore a coating of dust. She didn't even have flip-flops. If this had been the States, Dad would have reported her parents to Child Protective Services, because she certainly looked neglected.

"I help camp?" she asked.

"That's a great idea," I said. "Absolutely wonder-ful." Anything to get out of baby-sitting the five-year-old menace to society.

Mom and Dad looked at each other, then at Chelsea. "Well," he said, "maybe she could help."

"But doesn't she have to go to school?" Mom asked. "Surely . . ." She hesitated, looking at Nirmala.

"I no go school," said Nirmala firmly. "I help camp," she repeated.

When we reached the hospital, the head nurse shooed Nirmala out. In the reception room we were politely offered chairs. Then a couple of men made speeches, some in English, some in Nepali. They were probably boring in Nepali, too.

I did what I always do when I have extra time: I drew the scene in my sketchbook. Through the open window, I could see the top of Nirmala's head, her dark eyes taking everything in. I put down my pencil and waved, but she must have thought I was shooing her away, too, because she disappeared.

Finally, the speeches ended and the tour started. The hospital formed the letter T. Past the reception area stretched a hallway with five exam rooms. Beyond wooden double doors, the wards headed off at right angles, one for women and girls, another for men and boys. Metal bed frames topped by bare mattresses filled each room. Alicia, the medical student, asked about the empty beds, and Dr. Khadka told her, "You will fill them up." The tour concluded with the X-ray room and one that could be used for a pharmacy.

Dad flicked a switch, but the bare bulb on the ceiling stayed dark. "The electricity doesn't always work?" he asked our guide.

"This is Nepal," came the answer with a smile.

Chelsea would be in the way while they were setting up, unless I looked after her, Mom explained. I then explained to her how I felt about watching Chelsea, but apparently my feelings didn't matter.

Luckily, Nirmala was waiting when the two of us came outside. Chelsea and I namasted her and she namasted us back.

"How old are you?" I asked her.

"I am ten," she said. "And you?"

"Twelve."

"And Chelsea?"

"Five and a half."

"She is beeg," Nirmala said, impressed.

"Yes, I am beeg," agreed Chelsea.

I shot Chelsea a look that would have done my mother credit. "Do you have sisters and brothers?"

"I have five sister," she said. "I have no brother."

"Maybe next time," Chelsea murmured sympathetically.

If my parents found out about this, we'd be discussing family planning at dinner. At least here, everyone was medical, so it wouldn't be that embarrassing. "Will you show us the village?" I asked Nirmala.

"Yes, I show you things. You come."

"We already met Black Handsome," said Chelsea, skipping down the steps. "You don't have to show him to us, but maybe we can stop and pet him on the way back home."

"Black Handsome is the goat who lives at the police station," I explained.

"He is very handsome," said Chelsea.

"For a goat," I added.

Nirmala laughed. "You like Black Handsome?" she teased. "I arrange marriage between you."

"There isn't room in the tent," Chelsea said.

Nirmala's eyes met mine. I tried hard not to laugh. "And Black Handsome isn't old enough to get married," I agreed. Sharing a tent with my sister was bad enough.

First Nirmala took us to a fabric shop with shelves full of cotton bolts. A man sat at an antique sewing machine, pumping the treadle with his foot to make it go.

"You can have Nepali dress made, no?" Nirmala asked hopefully.

"Maybe," I said. I did not picture myself wrapped in yards of sari. I had noticed a few women wearing a long split tunic over pants, which looked more practical.

Up uneven stone steps, we passed by a metal shop, then a snack shop. Chelsea said, "I'm hungry." She had spied some sodas cooling in a bucket of water. "And I'm thirsty, too."

"I'll buy you a soda, but you have to wait for lunch to have something to eat."

"Okay," she said, for once agreeable.

I dug into my pocket for the rupees Dad had given me and bought three Mirindas. We sat down to drink them. Miraculously they tasted the way orange soda is supposed to taste. The plump woman who ran the shop shyly touched Chelsea's blond hair. Chelsea didn't try to squirm away as she had in Kathmandu.

"It's like we're Martians," I remarked.

Nirmala looked at me quizzically.

"Martians," I repeated. "Like from another planet?"

"What is, please?"

My first day in the village, I didn't think I'd be drawing the solar system in the dirt. I'm not sure Nirmala believed my explanation, and the woman who ran the shop had no clue what I was doing, for she had even less English than I had Nepali. Whether Uranus or Neptune orbited nearer the sun stumped me.

"But Pluto's definitely way out here. If I had a telescope, I could show you," I finished. "You can see Mars at night, sometimes Venus, too."

"I cannot come out at night," Nirmala said. "It is danger."

Did "danger" prowl outside tents where children whose breath smelled of chocolate lay sleeping? If something wanted to eat us, Chelsea was more tender and juicy. I could run faster.

"Well, I don't have a telescope anyway, but if I did you could see." Then I had to explain what a telescope was. Kind of like binoculars, and binoculars had been on Mom's list; I could show her those at the tent camp. We returned the empty bottles and continued exploring. There was a bank, a goldsmith's factory (three men sitting around Bunsen burners hammering gold into earrings and nose rings with spikes), even a small movie theater. "It shows movies from Mumbai," Nirmala said. "Lots of singing and dance. You like.

"On Saturday, there is a *bajaar*," said Nirmala, indicating the open dusty field.

"What's a '*bajaar*'?" I asked.

"It is a day when people come from the villages to sell many nice things."

Nirmala finished our tour by showing us the temple. On a stone platform sat a shiny brass statue. With its tail hiked up you could not mistake it for anything but a bull.

"That's a genuine holy cow," I told Chelsea, who still believed practically anything I told her.

"Sorry?" asked Nirmala.

"Just a joke," I said. "You wouldn't get it." I knew I sounded rude, but I was tired of explaining and it was better than admitting I'd been making a joke about her religion.

Nirmala still looked puzzled. "You want something? I get."

"It's okay," I lied. "I don't want anything." I'd like a friend, but selfishly hoped for one I didn't have to work so hard at talking to.

Nirmala squatted and pulled up a couple of weeds growing at the base of the stones. "Here. Take. Good in tea."

I sniffed experimentally. Mint. "Thank you," I said. "*Dhaanyabad.*"

Nirmala looked at me. "You talk English, Ahnee. I *learn.*"

That afternoon, the clinic started. I'd had plans to revisit the village with my sketch pad, but Tracey pulled me aside to ask if Chelsea and I would help her and Dr. Khadka, although I didn't know what use Chelsea would be.

"And Nirmala?" Chelsea asked.

"She's a girl from the village," I explained. "Her English is pretty good."

"Okay, then definitely Nirmala," said Tracey.

That's how I found myself demonstrating brushing and flossing to kids in line to get their teeth yanked. Chelsea handed out toothbrushes our dentist back home had donated, plus little sample tubes of toothpaste. Nirmala kept up a running commentary in Nepali, translating for those who didn't get it. She would get Chelsea to open her mouth, and the kids crowded around, marveling at her cavity-free baby teeth.

Tracey stuck her head out of the exam room and tugged her mask aside so she could talk. "Annie, are you free to help us in here?"

Nirmala had everything under control, including Chelsea, so I nodded and joined her. "What do you want me to do?" I pictured myself as a kind of dental Florence Nightingale, hygienically applying suction with a vacuum wand, when requested.

"We need you to help restrain the patients," Tracey explained. "It doesn't hurt, or not much, because we're using a local anesthetic, but some of the kids are still terrified." She paused and looked at me. "We need you to hold their legs, so they don't kick us."

I spent the rest of the afternoon draped across the legs of squirmy little kids. I had to sit on one with an abscess. By the end of the afternoon, Dr. Khadka was working exclusively on tricky adult patients, and Tracey was pulling teeth on her own.

"I always wondered what it would be like if I went to dental school," she told me when the light faded and we were all headed back up the hill. "I feel like I've had a crash course in tooth extraction." She thanked Nirmala for helping.

The girl peeled off at the bottom of the hill and darted into the twilight before I could say good-bye.

Chapter 4

I Go Back to Kindergarten

* *
* *
*

"**P**lease, Annie? It's only for a few hours. Then you can help out at the hospital."

Mom had sent Dad to beg me to watch my little sister. I spread peanut butter on my—well, it looked like a pancake—as I stalled. "How about if Nirmala goes? Chelsea *likes* her."

"Nirmala is too useful," Dad told me. "She's needed at the hospital."

I tried not to feel useless, but failed. Nirmala, along with a few rotating volunteers from the village school, translated for the medical team. They'd used adults, but the adults asked questions they thought the doctors *should* ask, instead of what the doctors *actually* asked. Forget that she didn't go to school; hands down, Nirmala was the best translator. Dr. Khadka told us she had helped out at four past medical camps, which explained why.

I gave in. It wasn't like Mom and Dad could call Grandpa to baby-sit. "Okay. Just for today." Another mantra, this one temporary.

I found Chelsea playing follow-the-leader with a grasshopper behind our tent. "Let's get ready, Chelsea. I'm going with you to kindergarten today."

"You're too big," she said. "Why do you have to go to kindergarten?"

It is easy to figure out why my mom needs a break from my little sister. "I don't have to go to kindergarten! I'm going to keep you company."

"I don't want to go," she said, suspicion in her eyes. "I went yesterday. I didn't like it."

"Maybe it'll be different today." Maybe you won't run away. Chelsea looked stubborn. "Come on, Chelse, how bad can it be? You like kindergarten at home."

"Well, I don't like it here."

I had to promise to buy her another *Mirinda* before she'd liberate the grasshopper. Fortunately, it was

32

easy to get her to brush her teeth, after seeing all those cavities up close and personal.

Stopping to stroke Black Handsome's silken ears made us late, but it didn't seem to matter. Although two stories tall, the school still wasn't one-tenth the size of Chelsea's elementary school, and Mom had said more than one hundred children were enrolled from kindergarten through sixth grade. The walls had been plastered with mud, which had cracked as it dried. I leaned over the closest windowsill—no glass or screen stopped me—and checked out the room: a desk, a chair, and two shelves of books. The library?

"Where's your classroom?" I asked. "Where are the other students?"

"We don't start here," Chelsea answered. "We have to go outside."

"We are outside."

"That way." She pointed around the side of the school.

The kids had lined up in columns behind the school. Waving their arms in the air to the beat of a drum, they didn't move their feet at all, maybe to avoid kicking up the floury dust.

"Where are you supposed to be?" I asked.

Chelsea pointed to a line of shorter kids, and we stood at its tail. We tried to follow along, but it was like dancing to an aerobics routine without the leader's instructions. Some of the kids turned to stare at us and got off beat.

"You could learn it if they do the same thing every day," I encouraged. Chelsea stood there, refusing to wave her arms in the air. If I didn't find a way to make her happy, I'd be stuck with her all day.

Morning exercises over, we filed inside. The kindergarten classroom turned out to be smaller than our living room and was wall-to-wall dirt. Some twenty kids crowded together on benches fronting skinny tables. Most looked kindergarten age, but not all.

A little girl with braided hair scooted over and we sat down. The teacher, Mr. Chobar, welcomed me as a special guest, then printed vocabulary words on the blackboard.

"B-R-E-A-D, bread! B-U-T-T-E-R, butter! T-E-A, tea—" the children chanted at the top of their lungs. Chelsea cringed and clapped her hands over her ears. She wasn't reading more than "C-A-T" and "D-O-G" at home. Certainly she hadn't memorized today's spelling list.

I tugged at her hands. "Just say the letters, Chelse," I whispered. "You'll learn the words eventually. See, you can write them in your notebook."

Next came math drills. These Chelsea could do,

though her zeroes morphed into kitties with triangle ears, long whiskers, and curling tails. Mr. Chobar pitted three kids against one another, to see who could solve the problem the fastest.

"Now, I hope Miss Annie will be the teacher," said Mr. Chobar, smiling at me. He handed me the chalk and the class cheered.

"What do you want me to teach?" I asked. I was not used to a grown-up's role—I was used to being told what to do. Not that I always liked it, but it was familiar.

Mr. Chobar waved his hands. "Anything you like. We are privileged to have you here." He gave a little bow.

I made a little bow back, then looked around for inspiration. There weren't any books, any maps, in fact, any anything. Fingering the chalk, I took a deep breath. "Okay, I have an idea. I'm going to teach you how to play hangman." I drew a gallows and six underlines for letters. "You guess the letters of the alphabet one at a time."

Some of the quicker kids caught on at once. I'd only drawn the head, the body, and legs for my born-to-be-hung stick guy, when one of the bigger boys shouted, "B-U-T-T-E-R, butter!"

The next one I knew only Chelsea would get.

"C-H-E-L-S-E-A, Chelsea!" she shouted. "That's my name!"

I drew a quick sketch of her face, and then I "hung" Mr. Chobar, exaggerating his nose and ears, and almost started a riot.

By lunchtime, Chelsea was giggling with the girl on her left, drawing a kitty on Manju's hand with a pen. Mr. Chobar would have to tell her to be quiet soon.

"That wasn't so bad, was it?" I said to Chelsea as we hiked back to camp.

"Except it's not like my kindergarten," said Chelsea. "They don't have paints or storybook corner."

"Still, I think you might like kindergarten now."

"I'm only going in the morning. Not the afternoon," said Chelsea in a determined voice. And since Mr. Chobar taught in Nepali in the afternoons, that was that.

Nirmala was eating lunch with the rest of the medical team when we got back. I loaded my plate with *daal bhat* and joined her.

"Maybe you will be teacher," she said, when I'd explained where I'd been. "I would like to become teacher."

"I think you have to go to school to be a teacher," I said. "Even in Nepal."

Nirmala studied her plate. "I used to go to school," she said quietly. She raised her eyes and they challenged me. "I will be teacher."

"So, why don't you go anymore?" I asked.

"Sorry?" Nirmala didn't understand.

"Why don't you go to school?"

"There is not money," Nirmala said. "And my mother needs me."

Mine had been listening. "I would like to meet your parents," she said. "Wouldn't you, Chelsea and Annie?"

I nodded, since my mouth was involved with chewing. I glanced at Nirmala, but she was staring at her plate again. Nirmala opened her mouth to speak, but whatever she meant to say got lost when Chelsea knocked her drink over. Sticky, lukewarm tea slopped over my lap, trickled down my legs and into my socks.

"Chelsea, you stupid-head!" I yelled, jumping up and plucking the soggy skirt from my legs. "Why do you *always* have to spill and why does it *always* have to be on me? Can't you watch what you're doing?"

Life is unfair. I ended up being the one who had to apologize.

I didn't want to spend any more quality time with my little sister, but after stomping off to our tent to change, the camp cook saved me. Naresh said Chelsea could help him, which meant she would ask a million questions and eat all his tomatoes. Later, during the lull between the chopping and cooking, they would play "I doubt it." Chelsea held her cards so that everyone could see them, and she lied *every single time*. I couldn't stand playing with her, but Naresh and his helpers didn't seem to mind.

"Please, Mom, I don't have to stay with her anymore, do I?" I made Frizz-spies-a-dog-treat eyes at my mom.

Mom smiled at her angel daughter, riding piggyback on the young man who carried water all morning up the hill so it could be boiled for drinking. "No," she said. "If Chelsea gets to be too much, someone can bring her to the hospital and I'll take off early. We could use your help, Annie."

So devil daughter was being given another chance.

I was looking forward to working at the hospital since I'd rarely seen my dad in doctor mode. Whenever Chelsea had an earache, all he did was rummage in the medicine chest for some leftover antibiotics, and when he couldn't find them, he had Mom call the pediatrician.

If I pictured myself working as a medical volunteer, I never imagined myself as Annie Ferris, Human Door, with the all-important job of deciding who got past me. Though, perhaps it beat tooth pulling.

The afternoon in a nutshell: my dad held clinic, my mom assisted him, and Nirmala translated. I ushered patients in and out, and ran errands. If I wasn't careful, everyone waiting to see my dad would come trooping in, privacy not being a priority.

First up, a baby with lots of itchy bumps. Looking at him made the backs of my hands itch. "Scabies," Dad said, and wrote a prescription plus told the mom to wash all her family's clothes in hot water.

Then came a whole family who needed deworming. We'd had to do that to Frizz when we got him from the Humane Society, but I hadn't realized it could apply to humans.

I placed my hands on my stomach surreptitiously. The possibility of a worm growing inside me didn't set well. Would it be like an extra long strand of overcooked spaghetti? Would I be able to feel it slithering inside me?

A man brought in his daughter next. She didn't

appear sick; she looked like one of the kindergarten kids. I took a closer look. She *was* one of the kindergarten kids.

I whispered, "B-U-T-T-E-R, butter," and she smiled at me. Her dad sat down and lifted her onto his lap.

Nirmala didn't have to wait for Dad because he always started with the same question. "What is the trouble you are having?" she asked in Nepali. I'd heard Tracey saying it over and over with each new dental patient.

The little girl spread her hands flat on the table. Along with the customary ten, she had two freaky extra fingers hanging by flaps of skin off the sides of her hands. Dad examined them, figured out there were no bones, and said he could take them off.

The father wasn't sure.

Dad said he'd use anesthetic. His daughter would be better off without the extra digits. They got in her way, flopping around.

The father was persuaded, and I forced myself to watch. Dad put on gloves, injected the anesthetic, Mom handed him sterile instruments, and I only winced a little when he cut. He put in two neat stitches, smeared antibiotic cream on the wounds, then stuck on butterfly bandages.

"Well, Annie, what did you think?" Dad looked at me. "You didn't turn green."

"I didn't pass out," I agreed. "Still, ew," I said, more for effect. "Is that what you do all day at your office?"

He said most American babies born with extra fingers or toes had them removed before they left the hospital.

I presented the little girl with a windup crocodile from our collection of fast-food freebies, and she and her father left.

I scoped out the hallway and what I saw made me queasy, for real. "Dad," I said, "I think you need to see this one next."

Dad got up and followed me. "Over there," I said, indicating a medium-sized boy whose lower right leg looked like raw hamburger.

"You're right, Annie, bring him in next." He said it in a really exaggerated calm way, so I knew it was bad.

His mother carried him in. The lady who had been next protested, but when she saw the boy's leg, she shut up.

"Annie," my mom said, "we're going to need hot water."

I looked at her blankly. The hospital didn't have running water, hot or cold. Then I remembered the tea shop. "Be right back. Come on, Nirmala!"

When Nirmala and I returned, taking baby steps to avoid slopping water over the basin's sides, Dad told us, "From what I can make out with sign language, he got bit by an insect some time ago, scratched it, and now has this major infection. He'll need to stay overnight."

Nirmala swayed a little.

The mother asked something.

Getting a grip, Nirmala looked at Dad. "She ask, will he live? Because if he will die, she cannot pay for hospital or medicine."

The room got still, and I held my breath.

Dad looked the boy's mother in the eye. "He will live."

I had to ask, though my voice got squeaky. "Dad, are you going to amputate?"

"Sorry?" said Nirmala.

"Cut his leg off," I said automatically. Nirmala sat down rather suddenly. On the floor.

"Whatever you do, don't translate that, Nirmala," Dad ordered. "I don't want anyone freaking out. Anyone else, that is." He wiggled eyebrows at me. "Annie, this is not the Civil War. We have antibiotics, remember?"

"Sorry," I said.

Mom rubbed hand sanitizer into her palms. "That's

enough for you two. Go back to camp. You can rescue Naresh from Chelsea."

Earlier I'd enjoyed being treated like a grown-up, but now I was glad to be a kid who could be excused and escape. I heard soft crying as we left, but I don't know if it was the mom or the boy.

I invited Nirmala to come with me. She hesitated, but I could be persuasive. "Nirmala, it won't be dark for hours. We can have tea. Seriously, you look like you could use some sugar." I could have added, you're too skinny anyway, but that would have been overkill.

I namasted the young officer by the police station. He kept a grip on his rifle even when Black Handsome butted him.

"I like this goat," I said, scratching behind his horns, then pushing him away when he would have chewed a hole in my skirt.

The officer muttered something. I caught two words, something like "*kosiko maasu*." I knew *kosiko* meant "goat."

"What did he say, Nirmala?"

"He said he is 'goat meat.'"

"What? You mean, they're going to eat him? Eat Black Handsome?"

"Yes, eat. Is good, goat meat."

I tugged on Nirmala's arm. "He can't do that! He's my favorite—I mean, Chelsea loves that goat. If she finds out they're going to eat him, she'll be devastated—" I caught the blank look in Nirmala's eyes. "I mean upset—I mean, she'll cry! You've got to tell him not to, Nirmala."

Nirmala looked at me like I was crazy, but she did as I told her. I caught a few words—*bahini* meaning "little sister"—more *kosikos*, and *chaina*, which meant "no."

When she was done, the young officer inclined his head in a nod. A smile peeked under his mustache.

"Did he say he wouldn't do it?"

Nirmala replied. "He say, he wait until medical camp is over, so *bahini* not cry." She looked at me out of the corner of her eye. "Also Annie *didi*, I think."

"Okay, you got me, Nirmala." That's the first time I liked being *didi*, the big sister. "You can't tell anybody," I said. "Especially not Chelsea."

"I will not tell," she promised. Black Handsome's stay of execution would be a secret we shared, just me and Nirmala.

Two minutes later, I unzipped the tent and crawled inside, calling to Nirmala to follow. I dug into my duffel and unearthed a dog-eared paperback.

"It's *The Secret Garden*. I've read it eleven times. I like it because it's not a normal book."

"Normal?" Nirmala asked.

"You know. I hate those books where the girl's biggest problem is that she isn't cool? Then something happens and she becomes popular overnight, but suddenly she realizes, hey, I don't need to be cool—I can just be myself. Normal books are boring."

Nirmala either couldn't relate or I was talking too fast. I guessed both. "Okay, never mind, but try this," I said. "It's my favorite. You can practice your reading, to be a teacher. It starts in India."

"Near Nepal," Nirmala agreed. "That is good."

We grabbed tea and biscuits. I read out loud, but the words were too hard for Nirmala, and she didn't like that it started with the heroine's parents' dying. We switched to Chelsea's picture book of fairy tales. Sleeping Beauty opened her eyes and Cinderella waltzed into view.

Nirmala thought those glass slippers were pretty dumb, too.

Chapter 5

All Creatures Great and Small

Never look down a tent latrine before breakfast. Trust me. All but one medical student was sick. Not a mystery—87 percent of all people who visit Nepal get diarrhea. Although in the case of the almost docs, Dad thought they were reacting to the local brew.

After I'd used the tent latrine, I saw Lance, the only one who didn't drink Tomba because it's against his religion, duck inside with his camera.

Tracey did a little dance, waiting her turn. Someone needed to dig another hole.

I nudged her. "Did you see that? What if he puts it in his photo album?"

Lance and my science teacher, the one who used to bring in roadkill for show-and-tell until a student passed out, okay it was me, had a lot in common. Kayla and I always suspected Ms. Koplonski took the flattened animal home to barbecue afterward. I resolved to give Lance her e-mail address. Some people are meant for each other and they would probably end up married. They deserved to be.

Tracey didn't answer. When Lance came out, she made a peculiar panting noise and bolted for the toilet.

I walked over to wash my hands. I pressed the button on the battered aluminum cooler, and water dribbled out over my left hand. I switched positions to get my right hand wet, then soaped and rinsed. I flapped my hands to dry them. You will not catch unfriendly bacteria colonizing around me.

Over by their tent, my parents were brushing their teeth. Dad spat toothpaste over the edge of the cliff, then turned to me. "Want to make rounds with me this morning, Annie?"

"Go ahead," Mom urged. "I'll walk Chelsea to kindergarten and meet you at the hospital later."

No Chelsea? "Time to go, Dad!" Before Mom changes her mind.

Tracey tottered out. Dad took one look and said, "On second thought, we'll start rounds here."

After dispensing strong antibiotics to Tracey, making her stretch out on a mat in the shade, and mixing up an anti-dehydration solution for her to sip—all of it, no matter how terribly grape it tasted—Dad and I headed down the hill. Dad was whistling. He says he caught all his bugs in med school, and I guess it's true, because I couldn't remember him being sick, except for the rare cold.

"Do you remember you used to make rounds with me?" he asked.

"Yeah. Wasn't it when Chelsea was a baby?" Probably Mom had wanted me out of her hair.

"That's right. Your mom wanted you out of her hair."

"You used to set me up in the doctors' lounge with my coloring books and crayons. There were jumbo muffins and all different kinds of soda in the fridge. You told me not to clue Mom in about the soda."

"Well, there's no doctors' lounge here, but maybe we'll get a soda after."

"Deal."

"But remember, don't tell your mom."

Nirmala was waiting. The three of us went into the men and boys' ward first. All six beds were full. Raw hamburger boy was sitting up, playing with a set of windup teeth. He sent them chattering toward his little brother's toes. Little brother squealed in delight.

"Obviously, you're feeling good this morning." Dad unwrapped the bandage on the boy's leg, and said to me, "This is looking good. People here respond quickly to antibiotics. No drug resistance whatsoever."

He put some cream on the boy's leg. "Would you wrap Ram Bhahadur back up, Annie?" He held out a roll of gauze.

Nirmala stepped forward. "I do it."

"I thought you wanted to be a teacher, not a nurse," I protested. Still, I was fine with her redoing the dressing, even if I'd let Dad down. Ram's skin looked so pink and tender I was afraid I'd hurt him, and it wasn't like I wanted to be a doctor.

Nirmala shrugged. "It is to be done."

My father gave Ram's mother the rest of the cream and said he could go home. We moved on to the next patient, a young man with a bandaged neck.

"When he came in yesterday, this abscess was the size of a golf ball." Dad held out his hands to show how big.

Dad gets excited about the weirdest things. "I'm not sure I wanted to know that. I bet you didn't either, Nirmala."

"What is this 'golf ball'?" Nirmala asked.

When he had finished explaining what a wonderfully exciting game golf was, Dad checked the young man's neck drain while I counted how many pills he had left to make sure he was taking his antibiotics. Dad got a syringe out and handed me a kidney-shaped plastic bowl. "This is hands-on medicine, Annie, and I need your helping hands. Close your eyes if you need to, but don't drop the bowl. It's important."

Before I could react, he started sucking a load of yellow pus from the young man's neck. He squirted it into the bowl.

Maybe there are grosser things, but I couldn't think of any. "Yuck, Dad!" I tried to stopper my nose by hoovering in my nostrils. I was determined not to screw up this time.

It took three full syringes to get it all. When he finished, Dad told the young man through Nirmala to get tested for tuberculosis. "One more day, then you can go home," Dad told him cheerfully.

We checked on the health of four more patients and sent three of them home, before proceeding to the women's ward.

Only one bed was occupied. "Did only the boys and men get sick this week?" I asked.

"I think that people don't bring their daughters to the doctor the way they do their sons," Dad said. He made a disapproving noise in his throat.

"That's the way it is at the school, too. Most of the students are boys. It's not fair." I looked at Nirmala for an explanation.

"Girls must help their mothers," she observed.

Yeah, right. Logic said since Nirmala wasn't in school, she should be home helping *her* mother. Obviously, she wasn't. There was a mystery about Nirmala, but also work to do. I said a little prayer that this time it wouldn't involve pus.

The girl lay with her leg in a hip-to-ankle splint. It had been padded with cotton and was held in place with duct tape. Some big pink pills lay beside her in a bubble pack.

My dad namasted her, and she shyly namasted us back. "For this little one, we are waiting for the X-ray machine to be operational again, before we put on a cast. She has a bad break near her hip."

I flipped the switch by the door. "Good news, Dad! The electricity's working."

"Ah, but the X-ray technician is not working today. He went back to his village."

"When will he be back?"

"Good question," my father said. "I hope it's not for an extended vacation."

Nirmala and the girl were talking, and before too long, Nirmala had her smiling a little. "She fell out of tree," Nirmala explained. "She says she will knock down the green mangoes with a long stick next time."

"Good plan," I said.

Dad and I moved away. Dad stood in the middle of the room tugging on his left ear. He frowned at his clipboard, as though he needed his reading glasses.

"There should be someone else here. A woman? A very pregnant woman?" He called Nirmala over and asked, but Nirmala didn't know anything about her.

"Maybe she's in the bathroom," I said. But she wasn't when I looked.

We decided to ask the head nurse. We found her in the makeshift pharmacy chatting with Kalpana and Devyani.

"The woman you are looking for has gone home," Nirmala informed us.

"When?" asked Dad. "Why didn't she try to stop her? She can't go home. She needs to have that baby in the hospital."

I think Nirmala had trouble following the pronouns, but she got the gist. "You want her in hospital?"

"Which direction?" Dad asked. "How long ago?" He does not give up easily.

There was some rapid back and forth between Nirmala and the nurse. We couldn't get a good answer about the timing; hardly anyone wears a watch here. Soon we found ourselves hiking up toward Manibajaar. Five minutes' walk and we were out of the village, heading up the dusty pathway before it split.

"You two go that way, and I'll go this way." Dad pointed. "Whoever finds her first, make her come back to the hospital."

Thankfully, the pregnant lady hadn't gone too far—she couldn't waddle very fast. She was sitting under a tree looking crabby at her husband. After Nirmala negotiated with the couple, she promised to return after resting in the shade awhile longer.

We rushed back to the fork and gave Dad the good news. "That's a relief. I've never had a patient run away before," Dad said. He wiped the sweat off his shiny head with a bandanna.

"But at least she's coming," I said. "Now she'll be all right. Won't she?"

"I hope so." Dad gave me a hug and a squeeze. Nirmala got one, too.

While Dad was buying the Mirindas, Nirmala looked at me seriously. "You lucky girl, Annie," she said.

"Why am I lucky?"

"You have father doctor."

"Yes, I do," I said, not quite knowing what Nirmala was getting at. At home, having a doctor for a dad meant a big house, a swimming pool, and private art lessons on Saturdays. I wondered if Nirmala was upset with her dad because she couldn't go to school anymore. I rummaged in my pack. "Let me draw you, Nirmala. Hold still."

But when I opened my sketchbook, I found someone had beaten me to it, scribbling five pictures of a four-legged grasshopper. That someone had also broken the lead off two of my pencils.

"Nirmala, you don't know how lucky you are to have only older sisters," I said grimly.

* * *

I cornered my little sister behind our tent, Nirmala hot on my heels. "Chelsea, you're dead meat! Look at my sketchbook!" I thrust it at her. "You drew these mutant grasshoppers, didn't you?"

Chelsea held the sketchbook by the edges as if it would bite her. "Maybe," she answered in a small voice. She looked to Nirmala for help.

"What do you mean, 'maybe'? It *was* you."

Chelsea looked scared, like she was afraid I'd clobber her. Good. "You're supposed to ask before you use my things."

"Don't be mad, Annie," she whispered. "I wanted to draw like you." She turned on the crocodile tears. She clutched Nirmala around the waist and wouldn't let go. Nirmala curved an arm protectively about her. "*Bahini*," she said. "You fix."

I felt very grown-up as I handed Chelsea one of my art gum erasers. "You erase very carefully."

A few days later, lunch was over and we weren't due back at the hospital for another hour. I dug some M&M's out of my duffel bag to share with Nirmala. Chelsea was there, too, but I wasn't sharing with her. Fortunately my personal chocolate supply was holding up. I had it well hidden.

That's when Nirmala asked Chelsea about her morning. Sometimes that girl is too polite. I bet they practiced tea-party manners in that school before she left.

Chelsea said there were hard words on the board, but that it didn't matter. "Because I'm never going back to kindergarden," she declared.

"What's that?" I asked. I was eating my M&M's in rainbow order, starting with red.

"Manju got a bad haircut, and I don't want to sit next to her anymore."

Since Manju was Chelsea's best friend aside from Nirmala, this was serious.

I got a good look at Manju when she walked by the soda shop with her mother. Manju didn't just have a bad haircut. Her head had been shaved. "She's like Dad's Mini-Me," I told Mom when we got back.

"Why do I have a bad feeling about this?" she said. "Chelsea, come here."

She only found two live lice on Chelsea, but they had probably already laid eggs.

"I'd better check you, too, Annie."

"Why? I don't sit by Manju."

"I know. But you sleep beside Chelsea."

Suddenly my head itched. A lot.

* * *

The next morning, Nirmala said, "You have *jumraa?*" She tried not to smile. Then she teased, "*Bahini* Chelsea likes bugs."

"Well, *didi* Annie sure doesn't! Nirmala, my mom doesn't know how to get rid of them. At home, she would buy a special shampoo to wash our hair. It's a kind of shampoo that kills all the *jumraa.*"

"It is no problem. I show. You use comb."

Nirmala and I went shopping and came back with a bamboo comb. Then Nirmala had Chelsea sit in front of her and inspected her hair. When she found a louse, she said, "Ah!" and squished it.

Somehow I did not think the comb-and-squish method would be popular back home. Too labor intensive, not to mention disgusting.

"Your turn, Annie," Mom said finally. "You check through Chelsea's hair one more time while we work on yours."

"This is the one time Dad's lucky to be bald," I muttered as she and Nirmala began going through my hair. I refused to touch Chelsea's hair.

"You could be bald, too, if we can't find all these critters," Mom told me.

Ha ha, very funny. She was joking, wasn't she? "Mom, you are kidding?"

"Think of it as an adventure," said Chelsea.

When our hair had been nit-picked over, Mom took us down by the police station to wash our hair. Cold water gushed out of a open pipe about chest high. Chelsea screamed as Mom lathered. She insisted on shampooing us each twice. Then she did herself three times.

At lunchtime, Chelsea sat by all the medical students and announced what had been found in her hair. It was pretty funny watching their reactions. Maybe they wouldn't think she was so cute anymore.

The rest of the day was spent washing our bedding. Chelsea was not helpful.

That night, I moved my pillow to the south end of the tent, so that my feet—sealed in socks and sleeping bag—rested by Chelsea's blond hair, which Mom had braided.

Even though she had to talk to my toes, Chelsea was still full of questions.

"Annie, why did God make lice?"

"I don't know, Chelse. He must have had a reason. Go to sleep."

Saturday was *bajaar* day, the one day we had off from clinic, when the *tudlikel*, the all-purpose field beside the village, the land that wasn't terraced for growing rice, came alive.

"It's like a flea market," I said, looking around.

"Only without fold-up tables and pickup trucks," Tracey agreed.

A small woven basket squealed, and a woman fished out a piglet and ticked off its charms to a potential customer, who started bargaining hard. Behind the pig seller, in a bigger basket, sat a baby, her eyes rimmed thickly with black. Silver bracelets encircled her chubby wrists.

"The kohl's to ward off sickness, and the bracelets make her arms and legs grow strong and true," Tracey told me, but I was barely listening. I sketched quickly, crosshatching the basket solidly on top of the remaining lines of one of Chelsea's grasshoppers.

A woman in a headdress and velvet shirt produced a fine rooster, who crowed away. The two of them ended up in the picture, too. There were also candy sellers ("purveyors of cavities" Tracey called them), along with ropes of tiny beads, wooden combs, shoes, and rice.

"Where are the toothbrushes?" Tracey muttered.

"Grandpa said we should be sure to bring back some souvenirs," I reminded my mother. "Besides, you know, the lice."

Mom made a face at the L word. "This is a great place to get souvenirs," she agreed. "See what you like." Then realizing what she'd said, she turned to Chelsea. "Not anything alive, okay?"

Mom bargained for a bunch of bananas, not one of them longer than her fingers. Chelsea and I each ate two. They were sweeter than the ones we got back home. Then Chelsea got permission from Mom to buy Baba bubble gum for her entire class.

Nirmala was sitting beside a woman and two older girls at the end of one row. "Nirmala," my mother called. "This must be your mother." She bowed deeply and namasted her. "And two of your sisters? Is your father here?"

Nirmala looked down at her hands, fidgeting with some purses fashioned from scraps of colorful fabric. "My father . . . he die."

I looked from Nirmala to Nirmala's mother, who was smiling shyly at us. Then I looked down, and saw that Nirmala's mother had a basketball-sized bump on the front of her. She was pregnant with her seventh child.

Now I understood what Nirmala had been trying to tell me, when my dad got us sodas, how I was lucky: not because he was a "father doctor," but because he was there.

The purses were lined with contrasting cloth and cinched tight with string. The tiny stitches were so fine as to be practically invisible.

It's not like I had to drop hints or anything. My mother bought them all.

Chapter 6

Teatime

* *
 *
* *

The following day Lance and I hiked over to the next village. It felt good to move now that my leg muscles didn't get sore anymore when I climbed. They were tightening, growing stronger.

We'd been asked to do student medical checks. Lance, the future poop doctor, wanted out of the hospital, and he needed an assistant.

"No pus, Annie," he promised.

Such a sweet talker. "What about Nirmala?" I asked Mom. It was past time for her to show up, and I was worried.

"Go on," Mom urged. "I'll watch for Nirmala,

and see she gets a good lunch after clinic." Food was my mom's cure for what ails you, handed down from her mom. According to her, you never solve a problem on an empty stomach. According to me, you think especially better with chocolate.

As I sipped my cocoa, I thought hard, then got this funny feeling: one way Nirmala helped her mother was by not being home to eat *daal bhat*.

When we arrived at the boarding school, the students were lined up and waiting. Lance hoisted an oval bathroom scale from his backpack and I held a tape measure, as he marked off inches on the wall. We did the littlest kids first. I wrote down their names, heights, and weights in a composition book with a snarling tiger on its cover.

I was good at spelling names now. Most were spelled the way they sounded, with an occasional silent letter lurking in the middle, like the h in Kathmandu. While I printed as neatly as I could, Lance checked eyes, ears, and skin, then listened with his stethoscope for a moment or two. Sometimes he asked me to make a note. I wrote "needs earwax removed" a lot. Earlier in the week, I'd been present when a "deaf" child had been brought to the hospital. And, lo, a miracle had occurred when Alicia dug out the wax sealing up his eardrums. How long would it take for my ears to plug up without regular baths? Surely years?

I was taller than every single student and out-weighed them all, too.

The last student Lance listened to was a girl my age. "Annie, write down 'EKG,'" he said.

Like they have equipment to do that kind of test here. Get real. It's expensive and it's for hearts. Any-body who's seen reruns of ER knows that. "You really want me to write that down?" I asked.

He tossed me the stethoscope. "Listen," he said.

When I put the listening end on the girl's blouse, her heart jumped against my hand, like a small frantic frog trying to pound its way out of her rib cage.

"Feel that thrum?" Lance asked.

I swallowed, trying to remove the sudden lump in my throat. I nodded—I didn't trust myself to speak then.

Lance smiled at the girl, told her she could return to class. She had to stop and sit to catch her breath on the way.

We packed up the scale, said good-bye to the teachers, gave them the list of students who should come in to clinic, and were on our way.

I tried to match Lance's long strides, but every so often had to break into a jog. "Can't you fix it?" It sounded dumb even as I asked.

Lance kicked a rock out of his way. "A surgeon can," he finally answered. "A pediatric cardiothoracic surgeon in a state-of-the-art medical facility can fix it during an intense eight- to ten-hour operation." He stopped and swore under his breath. "I'm sorry, Annie. I shouldn't have made you. It's just, I wasn't expecting to find something like that."

"It's okay," I said after a moment. "The sharing, I mean."

Then I told him about Nirmala's father. "Do you think he had an accident? Did he get really, really sick when the medical camp was stationed in some other village? Or, could it have been something like the girl with the jumpy heart, something that couldn't be healed without a surgeon and a modern hospital?"

"I don't know, Annie," Lance said.

"Yeah," I said. "Because it really doesn't matter, does it? Nothing's going to bring him back."

Upwind from the latrine, Mom and Chelsea were reading a book. Mom marked her place and waved me over.

"We've been invited to tea with Nirmala's family today," she informed me. "We'll go as soon as you're clean."

I changed my skirt, but not the bike shorts beneath it. No one would see them, so they didn't count. Mom stowed two water bottles in her backpack, along with a packet of biscuits and two precious packets of M&M's. She smiled at me. "A hostess gift."

"Nirmala and her sisters will like those," I said.

"Me, too," said Chelsea.

We hiked down the hill past Black Handsome, dozing at the side of the young police officer.

Nirmala awaited us by the fork in the path. "*Namaste*," she greeted us, and Chelsea hugged her.

"I missed you," Chelsea said. "You didn't come to the hospital today."

"You'll come tomorrow, won't you?" I asked. "I'll be there tomorrow."

"Yes," Nirmala said. "I come tomorrow."

"This is very nice of your mother," mine said. We turned right and started climbing toward Manibajaar.

Along the way, an old man holding a black umbrella halted in the middle of the path. We stopped, too, and namasted one another.

"You are American?" he asked. He had a faintly British accent.

"Yes," my mother answered. She was wondering where this was going.

"Why are you here? Do you trek?"

"No," my mother said. "We do not trek. My daughter"—she indicated Chelsea—"is too young for that. We are here working at the hospital. My husband is a doctor."

"You are doctor?"

"No, I'm not," she admitted.

"You are nurse?"

"Not even that," Mom told him.

"But you are educated?"

"Yes," my mother said. "I suppose I am."

"What to do about Nepal?" the man asked. "What is there to do?" His eyes were sharp. He moved the umbrella and peered up at the sun, hot and high above us. "It does not rain," he said regretfully.

"No," my mother said. "It does not."

"If it does not rain . . ." the umbrella man trailed off. "You understand? If there is no rain, there is no rice. What to do with the problem that is Nepal?"

What to do, indeed. I watched, wondering what kind of an answer my mom would give. Would people go hungry if it didn't rain? Could they starve?

But before she could reply, the umbrella man had another question. "You have no sons?" Again he had that tinge of regret in his voice.

My mother gritted her teeth. I didn't consider no rain equals no rice comparable to the disaster of having only female children. Mom wouldn't hesitate to say so, either, but I hoped it wouldn't be in a long and involved way. Chelsea had begun to whine.

But the umbrella man did not give my mother time to answer. "Well," he said, "some must have daughters." His mouth creaked into a smile. "And granddaughters." He saluted Nirmala, before setting off briskly for the village.

Nirmala giggled.

"Nirmala," I accused. "Was that your grandfather?"

"The father of my mother," she agreed, eyes dancing.

Nirmala's home was about three-quarters of a mile outside the village proper. She ran ahead to let her mother know we were almost there.

We namasted each other, and Nirmala introduced us all. "Laxsmi," her mother was called. Her sisters were Sunita, Parmela, Nisha, Shanti, and Chanda.

Parmela and Nisha, who had been at the bazaar, looked like they could be twins.

"You have lots of sisters," Chelsea said.

"Yes," Nirmala said, smiling. "And I have to call them all 'didi.'"

"Because you are always 'bahini,' the little sister," teased Parmela.

"But someday I will be a big sister, too, and then I will be called 'didi,'" Nirmala declared.

Laxsmi had water boiling for tea. The chia was spicy and hot, washing away the dust that clogged my throat. We sat in the shade of the house on a wooden bench.

I was reaching for a snack when Chelsea elbowed me.

"Wait for Nirmala's mom," she stage-whispered.

"Since when did you get to be Miss Manners?" I sent my mom an ESP message. The rule of waiting for your hostess to pick up her fork when there aren't any is a no go.

"Eat, eat," urged Laxsmi. "Enjoy." Nirmala's mother did not eat or drink with us, but Mom whispered that it was customary to wait until after your guests left to take food and drink.

We did get Laxsmi to try a couple M&M's, though.

She ate a red one first. Then she put a yellow one in her mouth. She looked surprised. "But they taste the same," she said. "I thought they taste different."

We all laughed.

Chelsea pinched me, but not hard. "Annie," she whispered, "you should draw them." She knew I didn't go anywhere without my sketch pad.

"May I sketch your daughters?" I asked Laxsmi.

"Skeetch?" Laxsmi asked. "I am sorry, I do not—"

"Draw your picture," I explained. "Watch." I pulled my sketch pad from my pack and flipped it open. With a few bold charcoal lines, I got down a quick likeness of Chelsea. I added Black Handsome, chewing on her skirt. Somehow Chelsea and the goat bore the same mischievous look. I'd drawn Chelsea so often I could do her really well, without looking even.

"Ah," said Laxsmi, laughing. "Yes, I like."

"You should be in the picture, too," my mother said.

It was like arranging everyone for a group photo. Chelsea hopped off the bench, and Mom helped me line up Laxsmi and her six daughters. I arranged them so that Laxsmi would be the center of the composition.

I took my time, not rushing. The finished sketch

was done in pen. Everyone crowded around to admire it.

"You're better than a camera," said Chelsea.

"Today you're my favorite sister," I told her. Drawings, if they're good, capture a little bit of their subject's soul. Maybe here that means karma. Whatever you call it, I caught it. In the picture, Laxsmi's arm curved protectively around her baby bump. The girls leaned in toward her, and it was obvious she was the center of their world. Only Nirmala, on the end, looked straight ahead.

Before we left, I had to do one more drawing, of Nirmala and Chelsea, Chelsea perched on Nirmala's lap. I titled it "Friends," then signed my initials and dated it, in case I'm famous some day. I presented both drawings to Laxsmi.

"And when you have your baby," my mother said, "she will draw the baby, too."

"I hope, boy," said Laxsmi shyly.

"You have a lot of girls," Chelsea said. "You need a boy baby."

"Yes, I do," Laxsmi answered.

Nirmala walked us back to the main drag, then said good-bye. Mom and I took turns piggybacking Chelsea for the last bit. The sun was setting as we neared the police station. Mom set Chelsea down and said she had to walk. Irritatingly, Chelsea's legs worked just fine as she ran to greet Black Handsome and told him what we had been doing all afternoon. Mine, after my hike of the morning and this afternoon, felt spaghetti noodlely.

Tracey called out to us. "How did it go?" She scooted over on the dining table bench.

My mom sank down gratefully. "It went well," Mom told her. "Nirmala's mother speaks English almost as well as Nirmala. Apparently, when she was in school, Nirmala, that is, went home and taught everyone—her mother and all her elder sisters—the day's lesson."

"Nirmala says she's going to be a teacher," I put in. "She must have been practicing."

My mom was looking at Tracey. "I wish," she said. "I wish—"

"That Nirmala could still go to school?" I asked.

"You took the words right out of my mouth," she said, tugging on my ponytail. "I have a smart daughter, too."

"But no sons," I said, pulling a sad face.

Both Tracey and my mom started laughing. "What if I got another one like Chelsea?" My mom faked a shudder. "There were ten grasshoppers in my tent after lunch! A zoo! No, two children are enough. And daughters are perfect. I wouldn't change a thing." Her face turned serious then. "Laxsmi needs a son, though."

"Why?" I asked.

"Because she has too many girls," Chelsea said.

"No," Tracey told her. "It's because her husband died."

"But what does that have to do with the baby?"

"Only a son can inherit the land and house," said Tracey. "That's the custom. It may even be the law."

"But that's not fair," I protested. "It's not."

"No," Mom said, "it isn't."

"But that's how it is," said Tracey.

After dinner, Mom said I should go to bed early. I'd had a long day is how she put it.

I told her about the girl whose heart jumped like a frog, and she pulled me into her arms and rocked me as if I were as small as Chelsea. I didn't mind.

I fell asleep to the *slap-slap* of cards and laughter. The medical students were playing hearts again, the kerosene lantern spitting and hissing next to them.

Chapter 7

I'll Take the
Tooth Fairy, Thanks

In the morning, when Nirmala arrived, I was ready with chapatis and peanut butter rolled up, wrapped in a bandanna. "Let's go to the temple," I suggested. "We'll have a picnic breakfast."

"Can I come, too?" Chelsea asked.

I had learned not to give her a direct no—sometimes it avoided a fuss. "Not this time," I said. "This time is just for me and Nirmala."

"I want to go," said Chelsea stubbornly.

"You have to go to kindergarten," I said. "Mom says so. Look! She's over there. I bet she wants you." I gave Chelsea a push in Mom's direction.

"Next time, *bahini*," Nirmala promised. "You come next time."

"Annie has to promise," Chelsea said, looking at me.

"Okay, okay. I promise," I said, forced into it.

We were both hungry, so Nirmala and I ate the chapatis on the way. When we reached the temple, we sat down cross-legged beneath the golden bull.

It was the first time Nirmala and I had been alone since I found out about her father dying. I picked a sprig of mint and chewed on it. "Why didn't you tell me?" I asked softly.

Nirmala drew her knees up close to her body and rested her chin on them, making herself small. "I think that if I do not say he die, he will be there when I go home. He is waiting for me. Every day I think this."

"That way you could pretend it was only a bad dream," I said. "Like that?"

"Like that way," she agreed.

"But it really happened," I said. "How did it happen, Nirmala?"

"It was bee. A bee bite him."

Whatever I had imagined, it hadn't been a bee sting, a little thing like that. "I'm sorry," I said. "What was your father like, Nirmala?"

So she told me. His favorite color: red, like the rhododendron flowers. The place he liked to go to think. How he and Nirmala tried to make a kite together from a picture in a book borrowed from school. His dreams for the family. For her in particular.

And as I listened I thought that if my mom or dad should die, I would shatter. Break into a gazillion pieces. I remembered when my grandma Katy died. I was Chelsea's age. Aunt Lindsey told me not to be sad, that Grandma was in a better place, but I'd kicked and screamed that Grandma's place was with me.

When she had finished, Nirmala asked, "Annie? Can you make picture?"

"But I don't know what he looked like," I said. "I kind of need to know that, to draw a portrait."

"I tell you," she said. "You draw." She had that fierce look in her eyes again, the one that dared me to mess with her. She had faith enough for two of us, so I opened my sketchbook, and retrieved my pencil and my biggest eraser.

"Let's start with the head shape," I said.

Nirmala closed her eyes and concentrated.

We were heading for the hospital when I had my big idea. "Nirmala! We should go visit your father's thinking place."

"Where there are flowers," Nirmala agreed.

"You should take me. Tomorrow. Let's ask my parents."

It was a plan. But, you know how your mom always tells you to wear clean underwear without any holes or stretched-out elastic? So in case you get in an accident and they have to zoom you in an ambulance to the hospital, you're (literally) covered?

Bet your mother never passed you a bar of soap and pointed out a handy flat rock. When you've got your Fruity Loomies all lathered up and you're kneading them on granite, I can tell you: holes happen. And the moral of this story? Don't get your undies in a bunch in Nepal. As Mom and Dad keep reminding me, be rubber-band flexible.

The Zen of Gumby. And it doesn't hurt to take a deep breath and exhale "Om."

That philosophy was fine the next morning when Nirmala, Chelsea (who didn't let me forget my promise), and I embarked on our adventure. Nirmala knew where we could see rhododendron trees flowering. Her father had taken her there last spring, all by herself, and Mom and Dad had said okay, because it is the official flower of Nepal, and if you don't see it, it is like going to Arizona and skipping the Grand Canyon.

Naresh packed us each a lunch, more hard-boiled eggs than we'd ever be able to eat, along with a couple twists of salt, beaten rice for a snack, chapatis with honey, a cucumber, carrots, and spicy peanuts. I tossed in a couple precious packets of M&M's to bribe Chelsea with (our stash was definitely dwindling), and more than enough water bottles. My backpack was approximately the size of the Hindenburg when we were ready to roll.

What I hadn't counted on was its taking four hours to get to the forest.

I looked at Nirmala. "I thought you said you'd been here before."

"Yes. I have visit. Very beautiful flowers. Only little farther. One half hour," her serene countenance promised.

Now, we would have turned back earlier, but I figured going down the mountain had to be quicker than slogging up it. We'd be home by dinner. And it was so cool in the forest. The wind wuthered through the trees, birdsong filled the air, and our feet shushed through a shag rug of pine needles.

When we reached the rhododendron trees, they looked like flaming torches. Nirmala kicked off her flip-flops and shinnied up a tree. "You are small," she called from twenty feet overhead.

"Don't even think about it." I made eyebrows of doom at Chelsea. Cupping my hands around my mouth, I shouted so my voice would carry. "What do you see up there?"

"Come! I see everything! All beautiful things!"

"I see her underpants, Annie," Chelsea whispered. "I think they have a hole."

I pretended to be setting a good example for my little sister by not climbing after Nirmala, but the truth was I was scared. That falling thing. Even looking at Nirmala made me nervous.

Nirmala descended, placing her feet deliberately, testing that the branch would bear her weight before switching handholds. She gave each of us a flower. They were a deep vibrant red, but didn't have any particular scent. We played tag and hide-and-seek among the rhododendron trees, both Nirmala and I politely pretending we couldn't see Chelsea when her little butt stuck out from behind a tree. Then we sat down and laid out lunch on a bandanna. I sliced the cucumber and the carrots with my Swiss Army knife. You would think, with as many attachments as they cram into it, that some engineer would have thought to add a vegetable peeler, but no. I did the best I could with one of the sharp little knives. Then, our stomachs comfortably full, we stretched out on the cushion of needles.

It felt like late afternoon when I awoke. I repacked the backpack, making sure the rhododendron flowers were on top so they wouldn't get crushed. I wanted to show them to everyone back at camp.

I nudged my sister. "Time to head back, Chelsea." She grumbled, but sat up, and we laced her size two hiking boots. Nirmala led the way and we started down.

Then I got this suspicious feeling. I started to think I'd seen that tree before, and maybe that one, over there. But then I wasn't sure. I mean, trees look alike, don't they? You know, trunk, branches, leaves? I tried to make my eyes a camera, so that my memory would be photographic, like a snapshot. I wanted instant insight.

There's a village close by. We walked through it. So why am I feeling like when we finally get back there I should ask whether they've lost their idiot, so that I can apply for the job? If I can't find it, that has got to be some kind of sign that I'm overqualified.

Why did I have to even think the L word? We're not lost. We can't be lost. Not here. They don't have Search and Rescue here. They don't have trained tracking dogs to put their noses low to the ground and find your scent. We really, really can't be lost. Do not hyperventilate when there are no handy paper bags to blow into. I am talking to myself, which would be a bad sign if I didn't do it all the time. The first rule when you are lost—not that we are—is don't panic. Easy for a guidebook writer in a cozy, well-lit office to say.

Next year for Christmas I'm going to ask for a global positioning device *and* a satellite cell phone with an extremely dependable battery. Not that I'm panicking, no. I know where we are. And if we should just happen to be pointed in the right direction, we are three hours from the nearest village, and camp is two hours beyond that. At least.

Okay, we are definitely positively absolutely lost. "We have to think this through logically, Nirmala. Look at the position of the sun or something."

Nirmala shielded her eyes with her right hand and looked over toward where the sun was setting. "The sun is leaving," she said helpfully.

"Well, where it is leaving must be west. This morning, the sun was over there." I waved. "East. And that means we have to go that way." I pointed southwesterly. "I think." If it came down to it, we could judge our direction from the stars—there's a reason they call it the North Star—but probably we shouldn't attempt to walk down a mountain in the dark. I reminded myself again not to panic, trying hard to ignore that little voice inside that said we might end up as characters in a *Reader's Digest* Drama in Real Life article, which, if you think about it, always has a happy ending, even though you have to go through a coma or an extended hospital stay first.

I turned to my little sister, determined to wear my happy face as long as possible. "Come on, Chelsea, let's go. We haven't got all day." I sounded like my mom.

"My legs are tired," Chelsea complained. "They don't work anymore. You carry me, Annie."

It could be worse. Couldn't it? "Come on, Chelsea. One foot in front of the other. Here, have another M&M. It's Kermit-colored, your favorite."

I was reduced to doling out spicy peanuts, which weren't half as motivating, when Chelsea exclaimed, "Annie, I lost my tooth!" She held both hands over her mouth.

I stopped, my legs glad for the excuse to rest. "Let me see."

Chelsea removed her hands. She opened her mouth and pointed to a bloody gap front and center.

"Guess what, Chelse. Lose a few more around it and you'll be a vampire."

"Really?"

"What is 'vampire'?" Nirmala asked.

Chelsea thought all sharp-toothed creatures were cool; she had a shark tooth necklace she kept in her treasure box at home, but maybe she wouldn't be so enthralled about Count Dracula, with the forest rapidly turning gloomy dark. I did know Nirmala wasn't crazy about the night, so I didn't bother to explain about vampires.

"You'll look just like one," I assured Chelsea. Then I played the distraction ace up my sleeve. "When we get home, you can put it under your pillow, and the tooth fairy will bring you some money."

"What is this 'tooth fairy'?" Nirmala asked. "It is fairy tale? Like *Cinderella*?"

"No," Chelsea told her. "She's real. You get a Sacajawea dollar for every tooth. And you get five dollars if the dentist pulls it out, because the orthodontist said to."

"Where's the tooth, Chelsea? You didn't swallow it, did you?"

"No. It's right here." She opened a grimy hand and showed us.

"You need to be careful with it. Put it in your pocket, so you don't lose it."

"Yes, we must find buffalo," said Nirmala. "Be careful it is not lost."

Was I losing my mind as well as my sense of direction? "What?" I asked.

"A buffalo," Nirmala repeated. "Where there is buffalo, there is buffalo dung. Chelsea must put tooth in buffalo dung and throw it over the roof of house—if she does that, her new tooth will come straight."

This was the longest speech I had ever heard Nirmala make, but I suspected she was teasing us. "Buffalo stuff?"

"Buffalo dung," Nirmala assured us. "It must be fresh."

Chelsea's eyes were big. She stared at Nirmala suspiciously. Then she turned to me. "Annie, I want to go home," she said. "I want the tooth fairy! I want Mommy! I DON'T WANT BUFFALO STUFF! BUFFALO STUFF IS NASTY!"

"We'll get home," I soothed her, hiding my own doubts. "We just have to walk a little farther."

"Only one half hour more," said Nirmala without prompting.

The sun had not only left; it had packed its suitcases and whistled for a taxi. It wouldn't be back until morning. Chelsea sat down, folded her arms around her knees, and refused to budge. Nirmala and I joined her under a tree. Unlike Buddha, I didn't get enlightened.

Well, maybe a little bit. Things that mattered to me a lot at home—like avoiding the torture of practicing the piano every day—in the overall scheme of things, they didn't matter. I mean, unless I am going to be a concert pianist, it didn't matter at all. Grandpa is forever asking me, "Is it going to matter in a hundred years, Annie?" and now, I could kind of see his point. Right now what mattered was being safe and warm. Nothing else. Trouble was I didn't have any guarantees on either point.

As if on cue, Nirmala began to shiver. Her thin blouse and skirt were not going to cut it.

We were lost, and it was dark.

Chapter 8

Witches Do Not Ride Broomsticks Here

Nirmala and I gathered as many pine needles as we could. If we piled a thick layer on top of us, it would be like sleeping in a haystack, only pricklier. I was taking my cue from Little Boy Blue; don't say you don't learn anything from nursery rhymes. I wished I had his horn to summon some helpful agricultural types. On autopilot, Chelsea stumbled after Nirmala, but still managed to bring back a skirt full of needles to contribute.

"Are we going to sleep here, Annie?" Chelsea asked. She was standing close enough to Nirmala to qualify as her shadow.

"Looks like it." I made my reply matter-of-fact.

"I don't want to," Chelsea said. "I want my sleeping bag and my pillow and the tent."

"Well, we forgot to bring them, Chelse. The tent wouldn't fit in the backpack. But, we'll be fine, all cozy under these needles."

"No." Her lower lip pooched out.

"Chelsea, it's like when Mommy and Daddy are gone and I'm baby-sitting you—you're supposed to do what I say—"

"—Or I don't get dessert."

"Right. Now, if you listen really well, and do what I tell you to, you'll get lots of dessert tomorrow. But for tonight, we have to sleep under these pine needles."

"I want Mommy," Chelsea said in a small voice. "I don't want you, Annie. I want Mommy."

Logic doesn't work on five-year-old little people, but often bribes will. "Look, I'll give you a whole packet of M&M's when we get back—*all to yourself*— but you need to sit down now."

"I sit, too," Nirmala said. "You sit behind me, *bahini*."

Chelsea's lower lip trembled, but she sat. I piled needles over her and Nirmala's legs. Then I doled out hard-boiled eggs. We ate them propped against a tree, and overhead, its canopy blotted out the stars.

I never knew it before, but there is something comforting about a tree firm against your back. This particular tree had been growing in this particular place for decades, maybe even Grandpa's will-it-matter-in-a-hundred-years. It was not going anywhere, and neither would we until morning.

"So a vampire is like a witch," Nirmala was saying to Chelsea. I should have known she wouldn't give up her quest for information. If she and Chelsea started comparing notes on Dracula, I would need garlic to hang around my neck.

"Kind of," Chelsea said, in answer to Nirmala's question. "Only the vampire sucks your blood. Witches just eat you. Children are like candy to witches."

Personally, I didn't see much difference between witches and vampires. Dead is dead, right? Whoops, I had forgotten about the undead. Do not think about the undead, I told myself firmly. That's being way too morbid.

"Witches come out at night," Nirmala presently said.

I tried to think of this as just Nirmala making

conversation. It had to be coincidence that the blackness pressed in closer. But then I considered, maybe talking out loud, for Nirmala, kept the vampires, witches, yetis—all the scary whatevers—away. I was kind of wishing I'd never heard of any of them.

"So do vampires!" said Chelsea. I couldn't see her eyes, but I'm guessing they were huge.

"Once a boy from our village was riding his motorcycle . . ."

"Wait a minute." This was too much. "Nirmala, there aren't any motorcycles or cars in the village. There aren't any roads!"

"Well, there was a motorcycle," Nirmala insisted. "It could ride on path." She stopped to see if I would challenge her again. She took a deep breath and continued. "He was riding home, and it was dark, and he felt someone behind him sitting on motorcycle. It was witch! He felt her hands around his—" She stopped.

"His waist? His middle?" I asked.

"Waist. That is word." She paused. "He knew that if he looked at her he would not be able to stop looking at her—"

"Why?" asked Chelsea.

"—Because witches are beautiful. If you look at them, you cannot stop. If he look at her, he crash."

"In America, witches are ugly," interrupted Chelsea. "They are!"

"Yes, they are." I felt around and patted her hand. I wondered what would happen if a supermodel helicoptered into some remote Nepali village. Would the townspeople run her out of town with pitchforks? Or would they force-feed her *daal bhat* until she burst? "But Chelsea, here they're beautiful. So, what happened?"

"Oh, he crash anyway. Go off road. Motorcycle die and he break two legs."

"That's all? What happened to the witch?" Chelsea demanded. I could see her point. This was rather anticlimactic. No veins punctured. No one got eaten.

"She go like smoke," Nirmala explained.

"Disappeared," I said.

"Yes, disappear," said Nirmala.

"What happens if a witch gets you and you don't look at her?" Chelsea asked. "What if you're blind? What if you don't know she's a witch? How do you know she is a witch?"

Nirmala listened to this waterfall rush of questions and wisely chose to answer only the last one. "Witches wear their feet backward."

"Well, that totally explains why they have to hitch rides on motorcycles," I said.

"And sometime, she leave a mark," added Nirmala. "Once my mother was late, when she was a girl, you understand, she carry water, and witch left mark. It is on her back. It does not wash off, even with Hotel Roosevelt soap your mother give to us. Hotel Roosevelt soap smell beautiful, make you clean girl, Chelsea. You wash with Hotel Roosevelt soap?"

"You can smell she doesn't," I said, and Nirmala laughed.

Chelsea laughed, too. "I am a dirty girl with jum-raa," she said proudly.

I woke once during the night, Chelsea squashed between Nirmala and me. The moon had risen. Nirmala and Chelsea were both fast asleep. Nirmala had her arms wrapped protectively around Chelsea. It was very quiet.

If there were any witches abroad, they weren't making any noise as they tiptoed around on their bare backward feet. I thought about Mom and Dad and how worried they would be. I hoped they pictured us curled around the hearth of some nice person's house.

I wasn't sure I could handle this alone. I said a prayer like I meant it. Then I drifted off again.

When dawn came, we were still snuggling, huddled together under our blanket of pine needles. When the sun heated the needles, we shoved them aside, stood up, and picked them out of one another's hair and brushed them off our clothing. Everything looked better in the light, more cheerful. We made a quick breakfast of the last of the hard-boiled eggs. I let Chelsea divide the remainder of the peanuts. We'd be at the village by lunchtime, so I wasn't going to worry. Lying to myself wasn't entirely satisfactory, though, even in a good cause.

"That way, I think." I pointed. "Nirmala?"

"Yes, that way," she agreed.

"Is it one of your half hours?" asked Chelsea. "Because if it is, I want an American half hour."

There is a song about the bear went over the mountain, the mountain, and all that he could see. We saw the same thing the bear did when we came out into a clearing: the other side of the mountain. Not the side we'd become familiar with.

"Okay, we have two choices," I said. "We can turn around and go back over the mountain and down to our village, because that"—I pointed—"is not our village. Or we can go down to this village. What do you think, Nirmala?"

"I am thinking there is not food and little water. We go down this way, not back forest. This way we not lose village."

That meant that this new village would never be out of sight, which had to be a good thing. "So we go around the mountain, not back over it, to get home?"

"Yes."

"Do you know this village?"

"No."

If I had been in charge of the Great Rhododendron Expedition from the beginning, I would never have gone without knowing how to get there, and more importantly, how to get back. But Nirmala was only ten years old. Then I realized that even if Nirmala had started out as the leader, I was in charge now. I was the didi, the older sister.

I hesitated over which direction to take, but not for long. At home we'd think twice about ringing a stranger's doorbell, but Nepali people loved children, and never did I underestimate the Chelsea cuteness factor. That blond hair (we would not mention anything that might be crawling in it) would be good for some food and water. "Okay, let's do it."

There wasn't a path, but the going wasn't rough, only a minimum of rocks, and all downhill. (That is the yin yang of Nepal: you are always going up or down, flat and Nepal being the opposite of each other.) After an American half an hour, we found ourselves on a dirt path. This was a good sign, but which way to go? Downhill. We hiked for another ten minutes or so.

Then I stopped, and Chelsea bumped into me from behind.

"What's that?" she said.

"It's a bridge." Or it was pretending to be one, suspended by wires. It sagged gently in the middle like a hammock. Two more wires, for holding on to, swayed gently on either side in the breeze. Through the wooden slats of the bridge (some broken, others missing in action), I could see boulders at the bottom of the ravine and milky white water rushing around them. Glacier melt. Right.

Nirmala, of course, was already halfway across. She turned and looked back at us. "Come," she called.

I was all for turning around and following the path back uphill. Eventually it would lead to another village, even if this one was in plain sight, because it would be really stupid to have a path to nowhere. Just as it had to be incredibly stupid to set foot on this bridge. In America, there would be a DANGER sign warning us away, and maybe a statistic about how many people had died here. In America, they have road improvements. They even have roads. What a concept.

My breath came faster, just looking at the bridge, and my heart revved up.

"Are you scared?" Chelsea asked.

Duh. "Well, I don't like falling," I managed to answer. "It's not my favorite thing."

"I'll hold your hand so you're not scared," Chelsea told me. "That's what Mommy does."

Behind us I sensed movement. I whirled and found myself staring into the deep brown eyes of a water buffalo.

Chapter 9

Mr. Buffalo,
Could You Please Move?

Okay, so uphill was out. I tried to remember everything I'd read about water buffalo in *National Geographic*. Nothing much came to mind except "unpredictable," because I don't read the articles, preferring the pictures and their captions. Nepal's version of the tooth fairy was big, scary, and hairy.

Even if you've seen pictures of water buffalo, or been forced to write a report on one for school, complete with pertinent facts, citations, and bibliography, you still are not prepared for one in your face. Water buffalo are *huge*. They are like the bulldozers of the animal kingdom. Plus, they have horns, long curving ones, which are extremely pointy, all set to turn you into shish kebab du jour. Any matador face to snout with a water buffalo in the ring—instead of the standard enraged bull—would pee in his tight pants before running for the hills.

Chelsea had wormed herself behind me and clung to my skirt. We backed up to the edge of the bridge.

"Is he nice?" she wanted to know.

"I don't know. I'd like him better if he was in a zoo, I think."

"Me, too."

I waved my hands abracadabracally, hoping to make the water buffalo disappear. "Go away," I said. "Shoo!"

The water buffalo took a ponderous step toward us.

"Please?" I squeaked. I risked a quick peek behind me. Nirmala had crossed over and was waving from the other side of the bridge.

I promise you, it's not heights that scare me. It's the falling part, those twenty seconds yielded to gravity before I go splat on the rocks. No wonder my feet froze in place.

"Annie." Chelsea tugged at my skirt. "Annie! We can't stay here! We have to go across."

Sirens and flashing lights were going off inside my head, making it hard to concentrate. My brain wanted to call for backup. I studied the bridge. It still looked scary. At the opposite end, Nirmala was performing demented jumping jacks, waving her arms wildly.

The water buffalo took another step closer. Drippy snot poured from his nose holes. A fly buzzed by his left ear. He slid out his tongue slowly and slurped up some of the booger juice. I shuddered.

That did it. Clearly we had a bridge to cross. Only Chelsea wasn't tall enough to walk and hold on to the wires at the same time. Yes, you had to be at least four feet tall to get on this ride. To my credit, I did not once consider ditching my little sister. Maybe she could have scooted under those horns, and she could probably run faster than the buffalo, but I couldn't do it. I couldn't leave her behind.

It's amazing what fear can make your feet do. "Chelsea," I said, careful not to take my eyes off Mr. Buffalo and his horns. "I'm going to pick you up. I want you to wrap your arms around my neck, your legs around my waist, and DO NOT LET GO. You understand? I'm going to walk across the bridge with you."

"Backward piggyback?" said Chelsea.

"You got it. Okay, let's do it."

Chelsea clung like a baby monkey to me. I had her slip her arms under the straps of my backpack. She wrapped her legs around my waist. I put my right hand on the guy wire and stepped onto the first slat. The bridge dipped under our combined weight. This would be fun at Disneyland, I thought. People would pay money and stand in line for forty-five minutes to do this.

"Don't look down," I instructed Chelsea (and myself). I took another step, then a third. The bridge bounced a little. It was so not getting easier.

"*Hasta la vista*, Mr. Buffalo," said Chelsea. "I don't need your buffalo stuff!"

Yeah, he could keep it. I concentrated on placing my feet as near to the center of the slats as I could. Seven more steps. The next slat was missing. Not helpful, but at least Mr. Buffalo couldn't follow us, if he had had any intentions that way. "Chelsea, I'm going to take a big step."

"Okay."

I brought my left foot down, and my right foot quickly after it. The bridge boinged bungee style, and swayed a little, but it didn't twist or tilt.

We were two-thirds of the way across when a wooden board cracked when I stepped on it and my right leg fell through the gap. I lost my grip on the right guy wire, and suddenly Chelsea and I were dangling from my left hand. Automatically my right hand wrapped itself around Chelsea. I could feel her heart pounding against mine.

"Chelsea? You okay?"

"No, Annie." She snuffled into my shirt.

"You're scared?"

I felt her nod.

"So am I. I can't hold your hand right this instant, but we're going to be okay. Now, you hold on tight and I'm going to reach for the wire and pull my leg up." I swiveled and grabbed the wire with my right hand. I pulled and twisted until my leg popped out. The bridge tilted sickeningly and my eyes got a flashful of sunlight glinting off the rocks below us. My foot started slipping. Thankfully the toe of my boot lodged against a bolt, and I skidded to a stop.

Slowly, I inched along. Right foot, scoot hands— first one, then the other—then left foot. Right foot, scoot hands, left foot. I did not look up, or down, or sideways. I focused on the wire. On crossing to the other side.

Nirmala's voice. "You are close. I take Chelsea. Bahini, let go Annie now." Chelsea was carefully removed. I heard Nirmala tell my little sister to let go, then, "Take my hand, Annie." I had to consciously will my fingers to relax their grip before I could remove them from the wire and grasp Nirmala's outstretched hand. I held on tight.

Right foot, scoot hand, left foot. Right foot onto dirt, scoot hand, left foot. Left foot onto dirt.

If I ever have a reason to run away from home, it is not going to be to join the circus. I am not cut out for the kind of career that requires you to wear spangly tights and perform death-defying feats. I fell to my knees and stretched out flat on the ground and hung on to the dirt, feeling my body sink into the dust. I'm on solid ground. Yes! Next year when I'm in seventh grade, I think I can safely skip the ropes course. Finally I rolled over onto my backpack and watched the fluffy white clouds in the blue sky. Nirmala's face blotted them out as she hovered over me.

"Well, that was fun!" I said brightly. "Let's not do it again!"

"Annie, you okay," Nirmala whispered. "You okay, Annie?"

"I am wonderful!" I looked back at the bridge. The water buffalo had not moved. Not much foot traffic would be going in the other direction today. He was as effective as any sign: BRIDGE CLOSED.

I reached out with my hands. "Pull me up!" Nirmala took my right hand and Chelsea my left and got me to my feet. My legs felt shaky and I thought about sitting down.

Luckily, the village lay just ahead.

"Civilization, hurray!" I shouted.

"Hurray!" echoed Chelsea. She looked a little pale and her freckles showed through the dirt, but she was okay. We were all okay.

Chapter 10

Things Go to the Dogs

The first house looked deserted, except for a few mild-mannered black and white goats loitering inside a rock wall. Chelsea, also known as the human goat magnet, ran up to the gate and stretched out her hand toward the baby she'd spied next to its mother. The curious baby goat started walking toward her, its mother hovering anxiously.

I heard furious barking from the porch shadows and a large black dog streaked toward Chelsea like an arrow shot from a bow. The goats scattered in all directions, but Chelsea froze.

There wasn't time to think. I grabbed my sister around the waist and swung her out of the way. Teeth clamped air where her arm had been.

Then the dog jumped the fence in pursuit.

"Chelsea, don't move!" I yelled. "Stay behind me!" I jerked my backpack in front of me as a shield. Ears laid back, the dog circled, looking for a vulnerable spot to attack, its low growl a constant rumble.

"Annie!" Chelsea screamed, but I couldn't take my eyes off the dog.

"Slowly," I cautioned her. "Back away slowly. Slowly." If she ran, the dog would be on top of her in nothing flat. I had to hope she could get to safety. While I hoped, I had to be bait.

The dog attacked, and, for its pains, chomped a mouthful of L. L. Bean backpack. It spat it out and lunged again, grabbing hold of the backpack and shaking it. Something flashed by on my left—Nirmala running flat out in her flip-flops. The dog discarded the pack to watch her, but soon returned to its circling.

Nirmala raced by again, coming closer so that the dog turned to contemplate the new threat. She drew herself up as tall as she could, stared down the dog, and dashed off, trying to draw its attention away from me.

It was working.

"Go, Annie," Nirmala said. "Go *now*."

"No! Stop—I can hold him off."

"Better dog eat me," she argued.

"Better dog eat no one!" The dog rushed past me, intent on its new target.

Nirmala feinted to the right, cut her speed, and froze, arms at her side. The dog skidded to a halt. It approached stiff-legged, sniffed at her skirt hem, then finally retreated. It sat down by the gate, fur bristling and teeth bared. I reached for Nirmala's hand and we backed away, keeping the dog in sight the whole time.

It was over. My legs shook and Nirmala's hand trembled in mine.

"Chelsea?" I called. "Where are you?"

We discovered her in a tree, hung there like a tear-streaked Christmas ornament. I reached for her, and she dropped into my arms. Chelsea wrapped her arms around my neck and wouldn't let go. When she stopped shaking, I pried her fingers off one by one, but I hugged her awhile longer. So she smelled and had crawly bugs in her hair—she was safe.

"Nirmala," I said, "thank you." It didn't seem nearly enough, but it was all I had.

"Nirmala saved you," said Chelsea, awed. "She did, Annie. I saw."

"Yes," I said. "She did." And for once in my life, I didn't want to think about what had almost happened. It was enough to be able to walk away.

"I love," said Nirmala, looking at me over Chelsea's head.

"I love, too," I said.

Four houses farther, a young woman sat nursing her baby with her back to the wall. We namasted, and Nirmala made explanations, heavy on the kukur totchka, which meant "dog bites." The woman asked a few questions, looking at us in sympathy. Then she stood up and handed me her baby. Startled, I cradled him awkwardly, bumping his head into the crook of my elbow. The baby's mom then bustled around boiling water and making chia. She gestured to us to sit down and rest. I did so, being very careful not to drop her baby.

He was little, too little to be frightened of a stranger, even one with such an odd pale face. He looked at me intently, his dark eyes registering no surprise. I think when you are so little, everything is new. You must have to learn to be surprised, as you have to learn to be scared. The baby blew a little bubble with his drool, which was kind of cute.

Then he let loose, his pee arcing in a little fountain over my skirt.

The woman looked embarrassed, but I laughed, and she smiled. Yesterday, a little thing like pee would have bothered me, but today it was a sign that nothing else bad would happen.

The woman filled our bottles with boiling water and, when they had cooled down, I loaded them in the backpack. My palm grazed against a torn place in the fabric, and I found a bloody dog fang embedded in the material. "Hey, look at this!" I said, holding out the souvenir. "If I can drill a hole, Chelsea, I can string it on a cord for a necklace."

Chelsea took it and dropped it in her pocket with her own tooth. I'm not sure, but I think she hoped to fool the tooth fairy later.

When we were ready to go, the woman stuffed Nirmala's head with reliable directions. I made Nirmala translate them into English and repeat them twice to make sure nothing important would be forgotten. None of this one-half hour business.

As we left the village, a man with an empty doko caught up with us. Observing Chelsea straggling, he popped her into his basket. He didn't slow down— she must have been lighter than his usual load. We made much better time after that.

"Maybe it would be better if we didn't tell my parents and your mom about what happened today," I said. "What do you think?"

"I think good," said Nirmala.

"They might get scared," Chelsea added. "I did."

"So did I, *bahini*," I told her. I wasn't afraid to admit it.

By late afternoon, we were approaching Nirmala's house. Shanti and Chanda came running out, exclaiming, and suddenly my parents were there, too, and Laxsmi and Nirmala's grandfather, and Tracey and Mr. Chobar. Mom hugged me so hard she almost squeezed the stuffing out of me. Dad was doing the same to Chelsea.

When Mom finally let go, she patted me down, looking for broken bones. "We were so worried when you didn't come back!" she was saying. "Don't ever do it again. Ever." When Mom was finally done alternately hugging and scolding us, Laxsmi brought *chia*. I blew on mine to cool it, then took a cautious sip.

"It really wasn't so bad, Mom. We did get a little hungry, but then a lady in the next village over gave us some *chia* and *daal bhat*."

"I'm glad someone fed you. Annie, thank you for watching out for Chelsea and Nirmala."

"Yes, it is good that," added Laxsmi. She stood behind Nirmala with her hands on her shoulders.

I wasn't about to hog all the credit. "Mom, it was more like Nirmala watched out for us. I didn't know what to do, so I just focused on one thing at a time. Like last night, we needed to stay warm, so we collected pine needles to cover ourselves."

"Well, one thing at a time worked," said Dad. "Sometimes that's all you need. If you can concentrate on the thing you need to do and forget about everything else, you'll do it. I'm proud of you, Annie."

Chapter 11

Thankful

*
*
*
*
*

Chelsea and I had agreed that what our parents didn't weasel out of us wouldn't hurt them—or get us sent to our tent without supper—but I wanted to tell someone about the water buffalo, the bridge of doom, and the dog who almost ate us. I picked Tracey.

She was doing her before-breakfast morning yoga stretches on a mat in front of her tent. Tracey is way too skinny to ever be mistaken for an ancient Hindu goddess, even if you added the extra two pairs of arms she'd need. She huffed and puffed her way through the poses as I told her about our adventures.

"So he didn't bite you?" Tracey asked, coming gratefully out of downward dog one vertebra at a time. "Not even a nip?"

I shook my head.

"You're absolutely sure, Annie." Her eyes bored into mine. It was an excellent look, one that would ferret out any lies about flossing only on alternate Mondays.

I could never get away with a fib with Tracey. "I'm certain. If he had, I would have to tell my parents." Though small, the green cartoon notices glued to the walls of the hospital had caught my eye. They pictured a man fending off a rabid dog with a long pole. I knew all about rabies shots. "The weird thing, though, was when Nirmala tried to get the dog to attack her so I could get away. . . ."

"I like Nirmala," said Tracey. She sank into a lotus pose and I joined her at the opposite end of the mat, folding my legs.

"Yeah, so do I. Uh, *Om*." I exhaled through my nose, copying Tracey. "But it was funny all the same. Funny in a peculiar way, I mean."

"But didn't you do the same thing for Chelsea? On the bridge?"

"Yeah, but she's my little sister. I have to keep her safe or I'm dead meat. But with Nirmala, it's as though . . ." I struggled to find the right words. "It's as if she thought her life wasn't worth as much as mine."

Tracey didn't say anything right away except to exhale "Om." Then, "Nirmala's attitude doesn't surprise me. That is the way many people think here. This isn't an all-men-are-created-equal-type country."

"But I'm not . . ." I wanted to say I'm not that way. I don't think of myself as better than anyone else.

But then it got all muddled. Because it is easy to think like that when you live in the United States and your water gushes out of the faucet. If I had to fetch water from a spring, morning and night, maybe I'd know differently.

Anyway, Tracey appeared to understand. She reached out and touched my hand. "I like you, too, Annie."

After I walked Chelsea to school, I met Nirmala at the hospital. Lance and Rudy set us to work inventorying the remaining medical and surgical supplies, then getting them organized. Everybody tended to grab what was needed, resulting in a jumble of bandages, tape, tongue depressors, and all sorts of surgical gear.

"Was your mother scared when we didn't come back? Was she angry?"

"She freak little bit, but she have prayer," said Nirmala. "It okay works out." She started working on scalpel blades. "*Ek, dwee, tien*," she counted out loud.

"*Chaar, paach, chha*," I finished. "That's six."

Nirmala gave me a sidelong glance. "I will be teacher when I am grow up," she said. "See, I teach you count already, Annie."

"I know," I said. "You will be a teacher. Maybe I can send you some books to read. I have lots at home, and I can always check out more from the library."

"I would like," Nirmala said. Then she asked, "What you will be, Annie?"

"I will be, I mean, I want to be an artist."

"You will be best artist. You already good."

"I hope so."

"When I meet you, Annie, you show me this Mars in the dirt and I think you go there."

Only if they put me in suspended animation so I can't think about what I'm doing. "I think I'm more likely to look at Mars through a telescope and draw what I see."

"This Mars, she is star close to Nepal?"

"And America. The whole planet. Only, when I'm home, we can't watch Mars at the same time."

"Why?" Nirmala asked.

"Because when you're sleeping here, I'm going to school in America. Your night is my day." I grabbed a lonely rubber ball from the toy box and demonstrated Earth's rotation, using the unusually cooperative lightbulb as the sun. Later, I said, "You know what else I'll be? Besides an artist?"

"What?"

"I'll still be friends with you."

Nirmala smiled. "You right. We are sisters now."

"*Didi* and *bahini*," I agreed.

Tracey came into the room just as we were finishing the inventory. "Are you two up for a little baby-sitting?"

"Does it involve Chelsea?" I asked, although suddenly I realized I wouldn't mind too much if it did. When I am an old lady with only dandelion puff for hair and Chelsea has a blue rinse brightening hers, maybe we'll finally be friends. Who knows? Perhaps it will even happen before we're octogenarians.

Tracey laughed. "No, but I've got a mom with a badly abscessed tooth and two little ones. Think you and Nirmala can handle them?"

In the hallway, a young woman sat all hunched over, cradling her jaw in her hands. A little girl who might have been four years old squatted beside her holding a plump baby boy. Risking pee or worse, Nirmala picked up the boy, and I took the little girl by the hand.

"Come back in about two hours, so Mom can have a nice rest. Thanks!" Tracey waved good-bye.

"Where shall we go?" I asked.

"To temple," Nirmala replied. "That is favorite place for thinking."

That was okay by me. I had some thanks to give for coming through our rhododendron mountain adventure unscathed. There are some people who say God is reserved for Christians, but I don't believe religion is discriminatory. The temple is a special place, and maybe that's where God hangs when he's in Nepal. When he isn't trying to protect mountain climbers on Mount Everest, that is.

I plucked a sprig of mint from the base of the golden statue, and we all chewed on a leaf except for the baby. He sat in Nirmala's lap, and pretty soon he fell asleep.

"You'll be a good *didi*, Nirmala," I said.

I asked the little girl what her name was, but she wasn't talking. I tried peekaboo and succeeded in coaxing out a smile, which widened substantially when I reached into my pocket and offered her some M&M's. Candy is the universal language.

*   *   *

When we returned her children, the young woman managed a smile, even though her jaw was swollen.

"What should we now do?" asked Nirmala.

"Let's go see what my parents are doing," I said. "Maybe they need our help."

My father was sitting at the desk in his exam room. In front of him he had his notebook in which he wrote down the names of patients and their diagnoses. He smiled when we came in. "Good," he said, "I was just about to start and I need my best translator. But I'm getting good now, Annie. Watch me. Sue, would you send in the next patient?"

My mom ushered in a couple. The father cradled a small child in his arms.

Dad was true to his word. In careful Nepali, he invited them to sit, and got their names and their village, which he wrote down in a composition book.

"They have walked far," murmured Nirmala. "Two day."

Then Dad tried to find out what the problem was. "*Pet duksa?*" he suggested. People's stomachs hurt a lot from worms, and he would dose the whole family, if that was the case.

The father inclined his head. No, not stomach then.

"*Coki?*" Cough? Many people suffered from asthma, particularly women cooking over open fires.

No, not that either.

Fumbling, Dad asked about itchy skin, but clearly he was grasping at shorter and shorter straws. The sleeping girl looked clean and well fed. Nirmala would have to take over.

My father warmed the business end of his stethoscope in his hands before placing it on the child's chest, so she wouldn't wake up screaming, but she didn't stir. Dad listened to her heart and lungs. "They sound good," he said. "Clear as a bell. No problem."

"See if she has too many fingers or toes," I suggested. He took a surreptitious peek.

"No problem," he repeated.

But the parents didn't look happy. Nirmala began questioning them in rapid Nepali. The mother answered in low, measured tones. The father interrupted and took over.

When they had finished, Nirmala turned to my parents. "She is asleep always," she said simply.

My father frowned. He took the child from the father and jostled her gently. She lay limp in his arms. "She has never been awake?" he asked.

Nirmala translated. "No," she said.

"She had no injury, particularly to her head?"

The girl's mother inclined hers. No.

My father said slowly, "It could be any number of things, not one of which is good."

"You mean she won't wake up?" I interrupted. "Not ever?"

"I would never say never, Annie," Dad answered. "But it's unlikely. Some kind of brain damage at birth, or perhaps the brain never developed properly in the womb." He passed the child over to my mother.

"This child is very well cared for," said my mother. "Please tell them, Nirmala. She is clean; she has good color. This is their only child? She has no brothers, no sisters?"

Nirmala inquired and the answer came back yes, their only child.

"She is how old?" my father asked.

The mother and father consulted. They came up with three years. Then the girl's father asked Nirmala a question. She looked at my father. "He ask——" she started.

Dad stopped her. "I know," he said. "And no, I'm sorry, there is nothing I can do. I'm sorry," he repeated.

What else can you say to people who have walked for two days seeking a miracle? I came up behind my mom and looked down at the girl's sleeping face. It was peaceful but blank, like a piece of paper with nothing drawn on it.

"She's like Sleeping Beauty," I said.

"In fairy tale," Nirmala agreed. "One hundred years she does not wake."

My mother smoothed the hair off the little girl's forehead. "Beautiful," she agreed. "I wonder—can you tell that story, Annie? Do you know it well enough?" When I nodded, she said, "Come, girls. We will go outside." My mother walked out of the room, and Nirmala gestured for the girl's parents to follow.

A large mango tree supplied shade and a waiting-room area for patients and their relatives, plus those who just wanted to watch what was going on. Since clinic was almost over, the space was ours.

My mother seated herself cross-legged with her back to the tree. "Begin, Annie," she said.

"Once upon a time," I said, "a very long time ago, a king and queen lived in a palace. They had everything they could want, except for a child of their own to love. . . ." I paused to give Nirmala enough time to translate my words.

Mom had me put extra things in the story that were kind of embarrassing, like how the king and queen tried to make a baby, and how to know when is the best time to make a baby. How the queen had to find a woman in the village to nurse her baby before she could have another. But the rest of Sleeping Beauty I told true, except for the part about the little baby brother.

When I had finished the fairy tale, my mother handed the little girl back to her parents, they put their hands together, bowed deeply, and said, "*Namaskaar*" to my mother and me. Nirmala explained that it is more formal than *namaste* and conveys much respect. We namaskaared them back.

"It is way to teach, to tell story," observed Nirmala.

"To be a writer," I said.

"It is good story. No glass flip-flops like Cinderella."

Later, the two of us were walking up the hill. Nirmala was quiet, tired out from all the talking. Black Handsome, that ungrateful goat, charged us, but I feinted and got beyond the length of his tether.

"You are a very bad goat," I said. "Maybe they should eat you now."

Breaking into laughter, Nirmala asked, "Where is *bahini* Chelsea? He miss her."

"Mom told her to take a nap, and she really is, I think. Our expedition tired her out."

But not that much, apparently. As we made a bee-line for the biscuits and tea, my little sister popped out of the tent. "Look, Annie!" Chelsea yelled. "Look, Nirmala! I got rupees from the tooth fairy! And I didn't have to do anything with buffalo stuff."

Chapter 12

A Too Soon Baby

*
  *
* *
* *

There was screaming. I sat up, but I couldn't see anything in the darkness. I struggled within my sleeping bag cocoon to free my arms. "Mom?" I called. "Mom! What's going on?"

"Stay with Chelsea," my mom ordered. She and Dad were strapping on their headlights, thrusting arms into jackets, rummaging for the first-aid kit. Mom whispered urgently to Dad, and they took off into the blackness.

"But I heard Nirmala—" I stopped. No one was listening to me. A kerosene lantern hissed as it flared up. Then I could see Lance holding Nirmala, who was no longer screaming. In fact, she wasn't making any noise at all. She flopped in his arms like a rag doll. The medical students gathered around, and I couldn't see her. "X-ray," I heard Rudy say, and their headlamps disappeared into the night.

Devil daughter wanted to leave Chelsea sleeping and run after them. She wouldn't wake up. What was wrong with Nirmala? Why did she need an X ray? It had to be pretty bad if it required both my parents and the medical students.

I debated with my conscience. Mom had said, "Stay with Chelsea." I could hear my sister's even breathing. I could slip away and she wouldn't wake up, but if she did, she'd be scared. Then I had a brain wave. Certainly I could stay with Chelsea if she was awake as easily as asleep, although I knew from the tone of Mom's voice, odds were high I'd get in trouble over it. I bit my lip. It was tempting. . . . It was happening. I felt around for my flashlight, rocked the switch, praying the solar-charged batteries would actually work. When the light flickered on, I took it as a sign.

I shook my sister's shoulder. "Hey, Chelsea, wake up! We have to go to the hospital. Something's happened to Nirmala."

Chelsea opened one eye. "You can wear your

pajamas," I told her as I shoved sneakers onto her feet and Velcroed the fastenings. "Hurry!"

For once she didn't argue or stop to ask a question.

In the exam room, Rudy, Lance, and Peter were holding an X ray up to the lightbulb. Gopal, the sleepy-looking X-ray tech, waited by the door. The medical students passed the film back and forth several times, Lance pointing to a particular spot. Looking pale, Nirmala was propped up in a chair, her arm held awkwardly in front of her. It had a funny twist to it that didn't belong there.

Lance spotted us. "Chelsea shouldn't be here."

"She's tough." I could vouch for my little sister. "We won't be in the way. Please let us help."

Lance looked at us. He nodded. Peter flipped open a medical textbook, but he quickly slammed it shut. "Says it requires reduction in the OR," he said. "Completely useless."

Surgery? That wasn't possible. Lance's expression didn't give anything away.

"Okay," he said. "Let's do it."

They laid Nirmala on top of the desk. Her feet hung off the end a little. I got on the side of her good arm, Lance on the other, not so good one, by her shoulder.

Chelsea moved into position by her feet.

"Where's Daddy?" Chelsea whispered loudly.

"He's busy," I said. "Be quiet." Then I focused on Nirmala. "Hold my hand," I whispered. "Look at me, Nirmala. Hold tight."

"I'm ready," said Lance. "One, two, three—pull!"

Peter pulled on her wrist, Rudy did something tricky by her elbow, and Nirmala screamed.

"Okay, X-ray that," said Lance. Rudy picked up Nirmala, Peter cradling her arm in place, and we headed down the hall to X-ray.

Fifteen minutes later, the three medical students were consulting over a new film. Nirmala lay on the desk. She was quiet, but her eyes leaked tears. I saw Chelsea give Nirmala's toes a kiss.

Rudy said a very bad word and the X ray fluttered to the floor.

"Give her another pain pill. It didn't work," said Lance. "Again."

"Nirmala needs a real doctor, not a pretend one," Chelsea said. "Annie, get Daddy."

"He's busy," I repeated, though I hadn't a clue what he could be doing that was more important than being right here, right now.

"Please be quiet, or you'll have to leave." I'd have

to go, too, if Chelsea got thrown out.

Lance bent down to look my little sister in the eye. "Chelsea, we *are* real doctors," he said. "We graduate right when we get back. Okay?"

"Okay," Chelsea said.

"Here, Nirmala," I said. "You have to swallow this. Open your mouth. It's going to be okay."

We assumed our previous positions. Nirmala screamed before Rudy and Peter even started pulling, then thankfully, she passed out.

"X-ray," said Lance curtly.

They say the third try's the charm. "That's as good as we're going to get it," said Rudy. He pointed to where two ends of bone kissed on the film. They overlapped, but not by much.

Peter nodded. "I don't think we're going to get better than that. Okay, let's splint it before she wakes up again."

"Chelsea, do you think you could fetch the duct tape?" Lance asked. Eyes wide, Chelsea did as she was told.

Once we'd seen Nirmala tucked into bed in the women's ward (she didn't wake up), Lance told us to go. We could come back in the morning. Chelsea and

I left the hospital, and stumbled back to the tents. I helped my little sister zip her sleeping bag, then climbed back into mine.

"Annie?"

"What, Chelsea?"

"I don't want to be a doctor if you have to hurt people."

"You don't have to be. Now go to sleep."

I must have slept, too, because I didn't hear when my parents came back at dawn. The medical students were talking about it at breakfast, which no one seemed to care for much.

Alicia was saying earnestly, "If she'd been in America, she'd have had a chance. Even maybe Kathmandu."

Lance said, "We all knew what the mortality rates were for women and infants before we came."

"Yeah," said Alicia. "We just somehow didn't expect them to apply to us. There's a difference between a statistic and a stillborn. You don't hold a statistic in your arms."

It was as if they were talking in some dialect I couldn't understand—I could catch words here and there, but not the sense of them.

"At least that arm will heal well," said Rudy. "I used the last of the duct tape."

"We've run out of duct tape? It must be almost time to go home then," said Alicia. She tried to smile, but it was wobbly. "God knows we can't do anything without duct tape."

Silence. "Does she know yet?"

"Sue's going to tell her later."

"Mom's going to tell who what?" I asked. "What's going on? Isn't Nirmala okay?" I was there. She had to be okay. I was the *didi*, the big sister.

"As far as her arm goes, yeah, she'll be fine. It's splinted, for better or worse, and your dad's going to check it later," Alicia told me. Then she looked down at her plate. "But, last night . . . Annie, your parents and I weren't able to . . . We did what we could, but . . ."

I stared. I knew then that Nirmala had been coming for help, only not for herself. "Nirmala's mother is dead?" I whispered.

"No, no, Laxsmi will be okay. But—"

I started crying then and Tracey came up behind me and held me tight.

Chelsea and I trudged behind our parents up the path to Nirmala's house. Nirmala wouldn't be there, I knew—she was still at the hospital, resting.

Sunita met us at the door and we exchanged quiet

namastes. Dad and Mom went inside to check on Laxsmi.

"Come see," said Sunita. Chelsea and I entered. We stood by the doorway until our eyes had adjusted from the bright sunlight to the shadowy room.

A kind of cradle swing hung in one corner. Sunita beckoned us over.

He was asleep. Fuzzy dark hair stuck to his scalp like ruffled feathers. His tiny ears had fuzz, like an elf's.

"He is so little," said Chelsea. "What is his name?"

"He is Rajendra," Sunita said proudly.

When Sunita had moved into the other room, Chelsea whispered to me, "I thought the baby died."

"One baby died," I said. "Laxsmi had twins, remember? She went into labor—that means the babies had to come out—but there was a problem— and they sent Nirmala for help. Only she fell, or tripped, and—" I stopped, my voice thick with tears.

Chelsea considered. "Do you think a witch pushed her?" she asked.

"No," I said shortly.

Chelsea stayed quiet for a few minutes. Then she asked, "Was I this little? I don't remember."

"No," I said.

"But he'll be okay?"

"Yes, I think so."

"Can we touch him?"

"Only if Dad says it's okay. You'll have to wait."

"Poor baby," said Chelsea. "Do you think he'll remember?"

"What?"

"Remember that he had seven *didis*, not six."

"I don't know, Chelse."

"It's hard to be happy and sad at the same time. We should just be happy."

I went to the hospital with Dad to check on Nirmala. She was awake, but lying in bed unmoving. Her grandfather sat beside her. He and my father exchanged greetings.

"Hi," I whispered.

"Hi," she whispered back.

"Nirmala," I said, "I'm sorry." I patted her hand, the good one. "But I'm glad for you, too. Your new brother, Rajendra, is cute."

"Yes, Rajendra is fine, and your mother is fine, all thanks to you, Nirmala. You're a real heroine. Now let's see if you can sit up," Dad said. "Have you been taking your pain pills?" He picked up the X rays lying beside her. "What do these have to say?" He studied them carefully, humming under his breath. Then he sighed. "Okay, I'm thinking you can go home now. You'll want to be with your family."

I found Mom in the tent, waking up from a nap. Well, I woke her. "Dad says Nirmala's X rays tell him her arm won't heal properly without surgery."

"That's too bad," my mom said fuzzily. She took a swig from her water bottle. She put on her glasses and looked more awake.

"She won't have full use of it, Dad said. Ever." I took a deep breath. "We should take her home with us. She could have the operation she needs there."

"Oh, Annie," Mom said, "I know you mean well, but this is her home."

"But the United States could be her home, too! She could go to school—you know she wants to be a teacher. How can she do that if she doesn't even go to school? Why can't we take her?"

Mom looked at me and sighed. "You're growing up so fast, Annie. But some things—some things can't be helped. She belongs here."

I argued some more but Mom was an unmovable force. I stomped off to my tent and zipped it shut so no one would bother me. I even pulled a sleeping bag over my head, but threw it off when I realized it was

Chelsea's. Frizz had needed me and I got to take her home. Why couldn't it be the same with Nirmala?

Because, a small voice inside whispered, it's not the same thing. Nirmala's not all choose-me eyes, licking tongue, and wagging tail, sitting in a four-by-four cage waiting to be adopted. You know it's not the same.

But I wanted it to be.

The funeral for Rajendra's twin was later that afternoon, down by the river. Nirmala stood with her sisters, her face set and sad, her arm bent into a right angle, all shiny silver with duct tape. Someone—it might have been Dr. Khadka—explained to us Americans that the river was holy. We stood a little apart from the family and the villagers, awkward, not knowing what to do or say, because we didn't want to do or say the wrong thing.

The tiny body was placed on the pyre. A man dressed all in white—I recognized Nirmala's grandfather—poured oil from a pitcher in a circle around her. Laxsmi and her daughters began to wail. The old man set the wood on fire.

It seemed to take forever. When all that was left was ashes, Nirmala lowered a butter lamp into the current of the river, and we watched until it was out of sight. It floated with the current downriver, careening along the sacred rivulets, bobbing up and down, somehow the tiny flame never extinguishing, as if to say: "Here I am, I'm alive, my soul is not gone, it is here, even though the fire consumes my husk, my shell."

It didn't feel then like any of us really believed daughters weren't important. Dad took me and Chelsea by the hand, and we watched as Laxsmi—carrying her one son—and her daughters walked slowly away.

A week later it finally began to rain, and everyone in the village ran out to dance.

Chapter 13

Oh, Mommy, Take Her Home

Half packed suitcases and duffel bags littered the camp. I could hardly believe we'd be leaving soon. Part of me wanted to stay—the part that didn't want to leave Nirmala—and part of me wanted to go—the part that wanted my own grandpa and my own dog and my own bed. And even though I knew that Mom was going to talk to Laxsmi, to see if there would be a way our family could provide a scholarship so that Nirmala could enroll in school again, it felt like being chopped in half. Only it was an illusion that the magician could conjure me back together.

*   *   *

Later that afternoon, Chelsea and I were supposed to be doing our own packing. But then we heard my mom talking. Tents are not exactly soundproof. And my mother was not exactly whispering, either.

"She said, 'You take to America. You have three daughter now. She your daughter. Take!'"

The two of us squatted behind our parents' tent, eavesdropping for all we were worth, our heads poked under the fly in the back, so we wouldn't miss a word. Now, I know we weren't supposed to do it. And I was probably setting the worst example for Chelsea, who didn't need any bad examples to pattern herself after. She was perfectly capable of inventing her own mischief. But this concerned us, too.

Mom must have paused to take a breath, because the tent was silent for a while. But then she continued, "It's what Annie wanted me to do, and I had to tell her no. But that was before Laxsmi asked me. Can you believe it, Kurt? How can we do it? How can we take that little girl away from everything she's known, from everyone she loves?"

"How can we not do it? You heard Laxsmi. She *wants* us to take her. She wants Nirmala to have the kind of future we can give her in the United States. What is there for her here?"

Dad sounded like he was getting into philosophy: the problem that is Nepal, blah blah, like Nirmala's grandfather when he stopped us on the path to Manibajaar. Mom hesitated and Dad pressed his advantage. "Remember what people said to us before we left? 'You're crazy! The children will catch some horrible disease.' How come no one ever told us the truth?"

"What do you mean?" asked Mom.

"The truth that we'd never want to leave. Taking Nirmala would mean we wouldn't be leaving, truly. We'd have something of Nepal. And we'd also have a reason to come back."

Again, silence. Then Mom said quietly, "I don't know if I can take her, but I do know I can't leave her behind."

I grabbed Chelsea's hand. Then I dropped it, because she had a grasshopper in her fist. I signaled her to follow me, and we made like snakes and slithered on out of there.

I stopped behind the latrine and turned to face my little sister. "What do you think, Chelsea?"

"About what?"

"Were you even paying attention? Do you think Mom and Dad are going to take Nirmala home with us?"

"To be my sister?" Chelsea said. "My *didi?*" She looked surprised.

"*Our* sister, *bahini,*" I emphasized.

"But I already have you." Her expression implied I was more than enough.

"Well, maybe you could have two."

She thought about it. "Okay. But only if it's Nirmala." Then she got a frowning look on her face and grabbed my hand. "You wouldn't stay here, would you, Annie? You're coming home, too?"

I pinched my nose. Porta Potties are a concept that will never catch on in Nepal. "I don't think it's supposed to be a trade, Chelsea. Anyway, I think I'm ready for flush toilets."

I ran to the hospital as if my feet had wings, like the FTD florist guy. Black Handsome looked surprised as I rumbled past him, a small part of my brain registering that he was still there, growing fatter.

The hospital was quiet. The patients had been sent home, somehow to fend for themselves, as there would be no doctor to take care of them after we left

138

tomorrow. Lance and the other medical students were packing up the remaining medical supplies, and talking about the first thing they were going to eat when they got back to America.

"Pizza, man, it's got to be pizza," Rudy was saying.

"Mm . . . with pepperoni and black olives," added Alicia.

"As long as the cheese doesn't come out of a yak, I don't care what's on it," Rudy declared. "Just the thought of yak cheese makes me want to yack. What about you? What have you been dreaming of, Lance?"

Before Lance could start salivating, I interrupted. "Hey, have you guys seen Nirmala?"

Lance fastened a roll of Ace bandage and tossed it in the box. "She's around here somewhere, Annie. Look around. And it's got to be mu shu pork, you guys. Chinatown, here I come!"

Tracey came out of the dental exam room toting a small box. "She's down by the wards, Annie."

"Thanks, Tracey!"

In the women's ward, Nirmala sat in the middle of one of the beds, holding on to a red plastic dinosaur with short arms and long sharp teeth. She made it hop across the mattress. I had never seen her play with a toy before. It made her seem younger and I could imagine her Chelsea's age. She gave a half sad smile when she saw me, and scooted over. I sat down next to her with care, so I wouldn't bump her arm.

"What are you thinking, Nirmala?"

"That I will miss my *didi* Annie."

So she didn't know yet about her mother's request. Well, I would not be the one to tell her because I wasn't supposed to know.

But maybe I could hint. "Would you like to come to America, Nirmala?" I asked.

She smiled. "Yes. I like visit."

"Do you think you'd be scared? I was scared when I came here."

"You scared?" Nirmala asked. "You not scared. No of bridge, no of buffalo, no of dog. You are bravest girl."

"I still don't like water buffalo. And look who's talking? You're not scared, either," I told her. "You're the bravest girl."

Toward midafternoon, Laxsmi arrived. She held Rajendra close to her. My mother joined them, and I slipped away back to camp.

* * *

A five-year-old can get away with things a twelve-year-old can't. Since I had dropped one hint, I figured I could drop another. I told Chelsea where I kept my Swiss Army knife and worked with her rehearsing how to flip out the knife without stabbing herself, in case she couldn't manage to untie Black Handsome's tether.

Chapter 14

In Nepal, There Is Always a Saying

*
  *
 *
* *
   *

We looked like we'd been in a bad accident, one with massive head injuries, but it was only the red tikka powder smeared on our foreheads to wish us luck and a safe journey. All the students and teachers from the school turned out to see us go, and many of their parents, too. They waved as we started down the trail to Tumlingtar.

Goats were cropping the grass around the plane. I saw they had a job to do—they kept the runway clear of weeds. Laxsmi was giving some last minute advice to Nirmala, staring at her as if to memorize her face. She tried to smile, we all did, but then there were tears.

"You are sure, Laxsmi," my mother said gently.

Laxsmi inclined her head.

"It is what my father want for me," said Nirmala. "I am ready for my adventure."

We climbed aboard and looked out the window. Laxsmi, Sunita, Parmela, Nisha, Shanti, and Chanda, with Rajendra in her arms, moved back, out of range of the propellers. They waved and we waved back.

Just before the door closed, my father got up and yelled something to them. I saw Laxsmi step forward, then smile through her tears.

"What did you say?" I asked as he buckled his seat belt.

"That she should come by the soda shop after the Saturday *bajaar*. They have a telephone."

Nirmala's eyes got big when we took off, and I clutched her hand across the aisleway. "We are like a bird," she said to me.

"Even higher than the rhododendron tree," I agreed. "What do you see?"

"All beautiful things," she answered. "This time, you see, too."

*　*　*

Later, Nirmala curled up on my dad's lap. Her mouth hung open in sleep. As I watched, he smoothed the hair back from her face, careful not to jar her arm, though the plane's vibration kind of messed up his good intentions. When we got home, Nirmala would have surgery to set her arm properly. But Dad had promised she wouldn't feel a thing.

In front of me, Mom and Chelsea were talking quietly, so they didn't wake her, although it wasn't likely with the pain pill she'd swallowed. They made people sleepy.

"Nirmala's never been on an airplane," Chelsea said.

"That's true," Mom replied.

"Don't you think Nirmala will freak out big time when she wakes up?"

"No, I don't think Nirmala will 'freak out big time.' You'll be here, and Annie, and so will we. We're going to be her family now, too, you know."

Chelsea thought about this for a while.

"Will we ever go back?"

"We'll have to take Nirmala back someday."

"I hope not for a long time."

"We'll see," Mom said. That meant it wasn't

something she wanted to think about right then. She wanted to concentrate on organizing the passports and the paperwork that would allow my parents to take Nirmala out of the country.

Chelsea stayed quiet for a few moments. Then she said seriously, "Well, I'm going to show her the barf bag when she wakes up. Just in case."

Behind me, Tracey was printing her address for me in my journal. "You know, Annie," she teased, "you're sitting by me. I thought you weren't going to do that."

"You're not going to scream, are you?"

"No. I promise." She handed the journal back to me. "Annie? You know what? Before I came here, I heard 'There is a saying about Nepal.'"

"And this saying says what, exactly?"

"This saying—" She laughed. "I don't know how long it's going to take me to speak English the way I used to again. Anyway, this saying—it says: 'You will not change Nepal. Nepal will change you.'"

"Maybe I saw that embroidered on a T-shirt in a Kathmandu tourist shop."

"I've decided to apply to dental school when I get back. By the time I graduate, I'll be approximately fifty gazillion years old."

"But if you don't graduate, you'll still be that old, Tracey."

She squeezed my hand.

It's funny. Tracey is my first adult friend. She's going back to Omaha, while we're headed hundreds of miles west. I'm sad, but it's not like when my best friend before Kayla moved, and there was suddenly a huge hole in the afternoon after school where she used to fit. Adults really keep in touch. They have e-mail. They send holiday greetings. I wonder if it's because Tracey seems like she's still part kid that I like her.

Because right before landing, Tracey swiveled in her seat. She spread her arms wide. "We're all going to live!" she yelled.

I flipped through my sketchbook. The last page I'd sacrificed to Chelsea. At first I thought she'd drawn a grasshopper, but then I realized the antennas could be horns. Black Handsome was eating grass under a rhododendron tree. Or a very large weed. It was kind of hard to tell.

"It wasn't just an adventure, was it?" I asked Dad.

He smiled. "No. Guess not."

Chelsea woke up then. "Where are we going?"

"Home," Mom told her.

Chelsea burrowed sleepily under the blanket. "Grandpa's sure going to be surprised."

Jennifer J. Stewart has traveled extensively in Nepal, where she helped tend patients in village hospitals and taught health education classes to women and children. She also trekked to Annapurna Base Camp and rode a runaway elephant. Jennifer is the author of *The Bean King's Daughter*, called "both amusing and engaging . . . fluffy and fun, with just the right touch of message" by *Kirkus Reviews*, and *If That Breathes Fire, We're Toast!*, which was selected for *VOYA*'s 1999 Best Science Fiction, Fantasy, and Horror list. She makes her home in Arizona. You can visit Jennifer J. Stewart on the Web at www.jenniferjstewart.com.